Bookman's
50¢
Bargain
Non-Returnable

**Stonewall Inn Mysteries**
Keith Kahla, General Editor

*Death Takes the Stage* by Donald Ward
*Sherlock Holmes & the Mysterious Friend of Oscar Wilde*
   by Russell A. Brown
*A Simple Suburban Murder* by Mark Richard Zubro
*A Body to Dye For* by Grant Michaels
*Why Isn't Becky Twitchell Dead?* by Mark Richard
   Zubro
*The Only Good Priest* by Mark Richard Zubro
*Sorry Now?* by Mark Richard Zubro
*Love You to Death* by Grant Michaels
*Third Man Out* by Richard Stevenson
*The Night G.A.A. Died* by Jack Ricardo
*Switching the Odds* by Phyllis Knight
*Principal Cause of Death* by Mark Richard Zubro
*Breach of Immunity* by Molly Hite
*Political Poison* by Mark Richard Zubro
*Brotherly Love* by Randye Lordon
*Dead on Your Feet* by Grant Michaels
*On the Other Hand, Death* by Richard Stevenson
*Shattered Rhythms* by Phyllis Knight
*Eclipse of the Heart* by Ronald Tierney

Also by Phyllis Knight:

*Switching the Odds*

# SHATTERED

# RHYTHMS

## A LIL RITCHIE MYSTERY

## PHYLLIS KNIGHT

ST. MARTIN'S PRESS
NEW YORK

This is purely a work of fiction. Most of the musicians playing in the Montreal Jazz Festival in this book have actually played there, but not at the same time, and not at the Théâtre St-Denis in recent years. The author wishes they would. André Ledoux came out of the mind of the author, as did the other characters, and any resemblance between his life and that of any real person, living or dead, is completely coincidental.

SHATTERED RHYTHMS. Copyright © 1994 by Phyllis Knight. All rights reserved. Printed in the United States of America. No part of this book may be used or reproduced in any manner whatsoever without written permission except in the case of brief quotations embodied in critical articles or reviews. For information, address St. Martin's Press, 175 Fifth Avenue, New York, N.Y. 10010.

Library of Congress Cataloging-in-Publication Data

Knight, Phyllis.
    Shattered rhythms / Phyllis Knight.
        p.    cm.
    ISBN 0-312-11888-0
    1.    Private    investigators—Maine—Portland—Fiction.
    2.    Women    detectives—Maine—Portland—Fiction.
    3.  Lesbians—Maine—Portland—Fiction.  4.  Jazz musi-cians—Fiction. 5. Portland (Me.)—Fiction.
    I. title.
    PS3561.N488S48    1994
    813'.54—dc20                                        93-45296
                                                         CIP

First Paperback Edition: March 1995

10 9 8 7 6 5 4 3 2 1

*To my mother,*
*Althea Rock Highlander,*
*with love.*
*With a great mom*
*you can do*
*anything.*

# ACKNOWLEDGMENTS
■ ■ ■ ■ ■ ■ ■ ■ ■ ■ ■ ■ ■ ■ ■ ■ ■

N othing we do takes place in a vacuum, especially creative endeavor. I have many people to thank for favors large and small, particularly the following:

Many deep-felt thanks to the wonderful pianist and singer Patti Wicks, who very generously shared her life and stories as a working jazz musician with me.

To Laila Begum for everything that's good in my life, and for taking me home.

Thanks to the Montreal friends who took in a Southern girl a few years ago and made her a member of the family. This is for you, too.

I owe a big one to the librarians at the Blue Hill Library for consenting to read a manuscript only two-thirds finished. You gave the author needed courage. Now read the ending!

To Norman Laurila, my agent: You've proved yourself a prince. Many thanks.

To Michael Denneny, my editor, for keeping Lil on track; to Keith Kahla for equal measures of wit and information; to John Clark.

To my two solid rocks in Montreal: Lawrence Boyle of L'Androgyne for his invaluable advice and interest; and Robert Lambert for keeping things HOT. See you in the Outback.

In addition, I would like to thank Jill Culver of the Hancock County, Maine, D.A.'s office; the women at Hancock

Travel in Ellsworth, Maine; Beth Bland; Rudy de Harak; Caren McCourtney; and Louise Bonenfant for her great idea.

I thank the people of Hancock County, Maine, for opening their hearts and wallets in support of my first novel. I'll never forget it.

And, finally, a tip of the hat to some fine musicians and friends whose dedication makes life a lot more beautiful and worthwhile to this music lover: Rich Latimer, Dawn Thompson, John D'Earth, Bob Jospe, Peter Dembski, and Charlie Pastorfield, to name but a few.

"What kind of singer are you?"
"I sing all kinds."
"Who do you sound like?"
"I don't sound like nobody."
　　　　　—Elvis at eighteen

To fall is nothing—but to get up!
　　　　　—old Amish saying

# SHATTERED RHYTHMS

# CHAPTER ONE

Y o u know, these days it's an old-fashioned concept that music can change the world—or at least some cynics would say it's a throwback to the sixties—but I believe it, I really do. Music goes straight to the soul and to the heart, with no stopovers, no messing around with the conscious thought processes and judgments that keep us apart. All you have to do is listen, and I mean really listen.

That's what I'd been doing for the past couple of months, that and not much else. When I'd heard that the great jazz guitarist André Ledoux was currently back in his home state of Maine, I'd decided to devote my time to catching him any place I could. I'd driven down to Waterville, where he was playing in the tiny Railroad Square Cinema; three nights later Molly and I made it down to Portland, where we saw him at Raoul's for five bucks. When he played at the Grand in Ellsworth, some friends and I were in the front row, cheering wildly. I even made a trip down to Boston to see him wow the big-city crowds, and that was exactly what he did.

Pretty soon, I'd covered three-quarters of the state and a good part of the rest of New England, and my heart was starting to lighten up from my recent troubles.

---

I'm a private detective. The Lillian Ritchie Detective Agency is mine, and I'm the *whole* agency, give or take some help from friends here and there, when needed. I'd started out for a different kind of life, playing the electric guitar in rock 'n' roll bands since I was a kid and writing the music I loved. After my early years in Virginia, I'd been headed toward the big time in Austin, Texas during the early to mid-seventies, when my closest friend and band mate was killed by a psychopathic drug dealer. I'd been accused of the murder and had taken that personally. To make a long story short, I'd finally helped convince the cops to go after the guilty party. But something inside had changed, something almost imperceptible, but there nonetheless, and I no longer wanted to be on stage. It was then that I apprenticed with a PI in New Mexico who taught me what I needed to know. I've worked at it for a while and make enough of a living to suit my needs.

In March I'd taken a case that initially involved a runaway teenager; it had seemed simple enough at the time, like many a disaster-in-the-making. As it turned out, I'd been forced to play a part in another person's death in order to save my own neck. True, I'd had little choice, and the man hadn't been much of a human being, but still I found myself besieged by guilt. It was what I'd done that counted.

You'd probably think that detectives would be used to death, but I'm not and don't want to be. So when I'd gotten back to Maine, bruised in body and spirit, André Ledoux seemed like a safe-enough bet. For three months, I'd taken no cases more involved than a divorce here, a small theft there. I'd thrown myself into the Ledoux magic like a starving woman at a plate of spaghetti. It had worked. Slowly, cautiously, I had come back to my world.

---

The phone woke me up. My face was mashed into the pillow and at first I couldn't make sense of what I was hearing. Air-raid warning? Had Saddam Hussein finally struck back? But that was crazy. This was the coast of Maine; he'd get

Washington first. But by the time I realized I had to answer the damned ringing thing, my arms were hopelessly entangled in a fishnet of sheet and blanket. I reached out blindly, struggling for release, and the phone landed on the floor. Damn! Another chunk of plastic had broken off. It lay there, accusing, like a knocked-out tooth.

I did a good imitation of my friend Dinah's telephone-answering etiquette. "What?" I shouted.

There was a moment's shocked silence. Someone cleared a throat. "Have I reached Lil Ritchie?"

You bet your ass you have, I thought nastily. Now live with it.

I sighed into the phone. "This is Lil Ritchie. Sorry about that. I'm not quite awake."

A pleasant male voice apologized for the hour. I glanced at the alarm clock on the bedside table. Seven A.M. Still practically the middle of the night.

"Lil, I don't know if you remember me, but we met at Raoul's a couple of months ago. I was playing bass with André Ledoux. We've spoken a few times. Ernie West."

I bolted upright. West was a fantastic bass player. Of course I remembered him.

"Ernie. Nice to hear from you. I'm just shocked that a musician could beat me up in the morning. Don't you guys still sleep 'til noon?"

He hesitated. "Sure, when I'm working. But we've been taking the past couple of weeks off, you know."

It was news to me. I waited.

He cleared his throat. "Look, Lil, there's something I'd like to talk to you about."

"Sure," I said. "Anytime. I'm always glad to talk."

"That's not what I meant. Listen—how soon do you get to your office? Could I make an appointment with you today?"

I glanced at the clock again. Still close to seven A.M.

"Where are you now, Ernie? I can be there whenever. My day isn't too booked.

"I'm in Bangor. I couldn't sleep and decided to take a chance on catching you early, before you got busy."

He'd done well. "Have you had breakfast? There's a little diner near my office in Tillman. I could be there in a half hour or so."

"That would be great. Thanks." I detected a note of relief in his voice.

I told him how to find Pat's. "If I can beat the lawyers to it, I'll get us a booth."

Some days, that's about all the challenge I can stand.

After we'd hung up, I stretched long and hard, then poked Littlefield awake with a toe, gently. I was taking a risk as it was. Littlefield's a black-and-white cat, lean and mean, primed for action. I had the scars to prove it. He cocked one eye open, then lazily closed it again.

"Okay, be that way. You can sleep while I have a delicious breakfast. You can always eat later." I sat up, as if to get off the bed.

I knew that would get to him. He stood slowly and then stretched his front legs all the way out, arching his back. He took his time with this, then crawled into my lap and I hugged him until he grunted, part of our morning routine.

"Let's go, Bud. The early bird gets the worm."

Littlefield glanced at me with what looked like disgust. I think his heart was set on the bird.

---

Pat's Diner sat on a busy corner, in one of the oldest buildings in town. It catered to the people who worked and lived nearby, which gave the place its charm. Lawyers with business in the courthouse up the street rubbed shoulders with blue-collar laborers who did hard physical work for their money and had the dirty uniforms to prove it; guys from the shell-

4

fish-packing plant and mechanics from the car dealerships below the river made the place a part of their daily routine; elderly women from the apartment building down the street came in for breakfast and the paper, knowing they'd be greeted by name at least once in their day. There weren't enough places like it left anymore.

The good smells nearly knocked me down when I opened the side door. By God, I was hungry. I looked around; there was one empty booth. Two lawyers who'd used the front entrance noticed it at about the same time. Race you for it, I thought. I slid into the low seat a second ahead of the fastest three-piece. He eyed me with what he thought was his mean look. I smiled my best smile and stuck out a sneakered foot for inspection. "New Balance," I said. "They're faster than wing tips. Better traction." He pretended not to hear and headed for a table on the other side. Some people have no sense of humor.

I opened the menu, though I seldom varied my breakfast order: ham and eggs, sunny-side up, with a biscuit, keep the coffee coming. Dot had noticed my arrival and was already on her way with a pot of steaming coffee.

"Morning, Lil," she said cheerily. "Whatcha doing up so early? Gonna ruin your reputation if you're not careful."

My waitress knew the real me. "I know, Dot. I feel my moral fiber fraying even as we speak."

She leaned toward me, her voice lowered conspiratorially. "Don't you know better than to say the *f* word in here? We're the last oasis in fiberland, and we're holding out the best we can." She laughed her musical laugh. "Now what can I get ya?"

"Coffee for now, I guess; I'm waiting for someone. Then I'll have my usual."

She smiled. "I knew you'd say that, but I had to ask, didn't I?"

After she left, I toyed with my spoon and thought about

5

Ernie West and what he could possibly want with me. With musicians, it was hard to tell. Someone slipped a quarter into the jukebox and "Little Wing" floated over and around the room, Hendrix's gentle voice smoothing down the rough edges of this morning.

As I sipped the strong coffee, I mused about what it would've been like if people like Jimi Hendrix and Janis Joplin had decided to live long enough for their music to mellow and deepen as they got older. What they'd left us was the sweet spark of inspiration, the raw material of youth, but I knew as well as anyone that there was much more talent there, waiting to be mined. Janis's last album, *Pearl,* had already given some indication of this. I didn't dwell on it, but sometimes I still felt cheated by the deaths of so many musicians, among the best of my generation. Why weren't they out there right now, singing and playing, helping us with life in the nineties?

I drained my cup. Some people are cheery in the morning; others get maudlin.

A moment later, I heard the screen door close behind me, and this time it wasn't just another lawyer. I turned around and saw Ernie West standing uncertainly inside the door, eyes darting around the room as if they had a life of their own.

"Ernie—over here." I stood up to greet him. We shook hands and slid into the booth.

As Dot brought coffee, I looked him over quickly. He was taller than I remembered, a good six two or so. His hair and mustache were reddish blond, and he'd recently spent some time in the sun, a rarity among musicians I've known. He had soulful blue eyes. I liked his hands—large and strong-looking, which they needed to be to wrestle with the thick bass strings night after night. He caught me looking and smiled shyly. "I guess you're wondering why on earth I called you. I really am sorry I woke you up, by the way."

It was my turn to smile at him. "It's okay, Ernie. I've been a little lazy recently, is all. When I'm working full-time I'm usually up by seven. But you're right about one thing: I'm curious about why you wanted to talk with me."

I took a sip of coffee and waited. One thing I know all about is waiting—in this business, people aren't always quick to come to the point.

Dot started over to take our orders, but I motioned her away for the moment. The man was struggling to find the words he needed.

"I want to hire you, Lil. I don't know any other private detectives, and I've been thinking about this for a few days. I'm prepared to pay whatever you charge." His voice was husky, as if he was talking through a lump in his throat.

"Hire me for what purpose, Ernie?" Not many people actually need a detective to solve their problems; maybe I could give him a little friendly free advice and send him home with his bank account intact.

He fiddled with the turquoise ring he wore on the ring finger of his right hand, then he picked up his coffee cup and sloshed the dregs around for a while. When he finally set the cup back down, I noticed his hand was shaking. He looked at me and I could see the worry in his eyes; blue eyes can't hide.

He spoke all of a sudden, his words in a rush to leave his mouth. "Lil, you've gotta help me. I think André is in trouble."

"What kind of trouble?"

"Well, he started acting weird a couple of weeks ago. We'd finished a gig in Augusta that had gone pretty smoothly, or at least I thought so. Afterward, we were sitting around, running through the evening, you know, letting off some steam, and André started acting bizarre all of a sudden. If I hadn't known he was clean, I would've suspected he'd taken some potent shit."

I nodded. I'd heard the rumors through the years of his

drugging and drinking, although the times I'd seen him he'd seemed straight enough.

"How'd he act?"

"Like somebody with a hit of bad acid. I thought he was kidding around until I realized something was wrong. He was acting paranoid as hell all of a sudden. I tried to calm him down, but he wouldn't let me. He knocked a table over staggering out of the club. I got up to follow him, but he'd disappeared. He didn't show up at his house until the next afternoon."

I thought that one over. "Has he ever done anything like this before?"

He smiled sadly. "When he was shooting up, he did plenty of weird things, but this seemed different. He's a supergentle guy, even on drugs and liquor. He just likes to go inside himself. Usually."

"I know the type. They worry their friends to death, am I right?"

West shrugged. "I've stuck by him through the years. A lot of his friends have, because he's such a wonderful person. He'd give you his last cent if he thought you needed it more than he did."

"So what's different now? I don't see what you need a private detective for, Ernie. It sounds as though he just had a little slip." I watched him for a reaction. It was then I knew he had more to tell.

He looked down at his hands, still holding the coffee cup. "Whatever happened that night seemed to trigger some other stuff. A couple of days later he was drinking again. I could smell it. That's always a bad sign. Then he got remote, the way he gets when he's on something. He canceled our gig at Raoul's, and another one at the university. Then, a couple of days ago, he took off. His wife called me, all hysterical, and I went over there to see what was going on. He'd taken his overnight bag and the car without saying a word."

8

"Maybe he's off somewhere by himself, trying to get his shit together. Maybe he just needs some time alone."

West shook his head hard. "There's more. His brother-in-law says that André came by on his way out of town and stole some money he had in a box hidden in a closet. Over a thousand dollars is missing."

Now this was indeed different. A thousand dollars and up, it's a felony rap, bad news all around.

I thought for a minute. "You said his brother-in-law. Is this his sister's husband or his wife's brother?"

"It's his sister's husband. I don't know the guy that well, but I do know he's hopping mad right now, and I can't say I blame him. I'm plenty worried. None of this is like André. He'd gotten his life back together the last couple of years, and I felt sure it was gonna stay that way."

I glanced away for a second to get my bearings, and the light in the room suddenly seemed brighter, the talk more distinct, the smells in the diner sharper, better defined.

The next thing I knew, I found myself saying the six magic words that have turned my life upside down more times than I like to count.

"What can I do to help?"

There. I'd done it. With very little conscious thought, the Lillian Ritchie Detective Agency was back in business.

West took a deep breath, his grateful smile beaming forth its considerable warmth. Under other circumstances, it would have brightened my day.

"Let's get something to eat first," I said, signaling finally for Dot. I hate bad news on an empty stomach.

---

Fifteen minutes later, the jukebox sprang back into life with one of Hank Williams, Jr.'s drinking, smoking, and whoring songs. I looked at Ernie, and for a second I experienced a mental short circuit. It was all too strange—an old rocker and a jazz musician sitting in a diner listening to Hank Junior as he bragged about kicking butt. The younger Hank had always reminded me of the boys I'd dodged in high school, the ones who spat tobacco out of the school bus window and laughed as it landed on someone's face. I suspected that, to some, that was part of Hank's charm. It was lost on me. Ernie eyed me curiously.

I shook my head and sighed. "You don't wanna know." I signaled for the bill. "My office is just half a block away. Why don't we move this up the street? I don't know about you, but I could use some quiet."

# CHAPTER TWO

The walk up to my office took only a few minutes, and we made it in silence, like a couple of monks practicing walking meditation. It was a beautiful morning, with the heat of the day just starting to build up. It was going to be a hot one. On the sidewalk outside Pat's, I looked up for no reason and noticed an eagle circling lazily in the sky above Main Street. I motioned to Ernie, and we watched the eagle soar higher and higher, in circles, until it flew out of sight. It was a common-enough occurrence here on the coast, but I'd never taken it for granted. We stood there for a few heartbeats, waiting for the dot in the sky to reappear and turn once again into a bird, but it was gone, so we moved on.

My office is nothing fancy, just a medium-sized second-floor room with a creaky old leather chair for my use, a much-used wooden desk, some file cabinets, a coatrack, and a couple of folding metal chairs for clients. Like a lot of private detectives, I do most of my work outside the office, so I've never felt the need to invest much in fixing the place up. I have a fine view of Main Street and the rooftops above it, which, to me, makes this as good a space as any.

I slid my butt into its favorite chair. I was ready for business.

"Ernie, exactly what do you want me to do for you? If the brother-in-law's as mad as you say, he's probably called the cops by now."

He shook his head. "I don't think so. Lucie, the sister, is real close to André, and I don't think she'd let Carl turn him in right now. I don't know how long she can control him, though. He seems like a real hardhead."

I'd been thinking about that. "Not too many people would tolerate having their money stolen out of their own home, family member or no. You wouldn't have to be a hardhead to be pissed about that."

Ernie shrugged. "I'd just hoped you could find André before this thing got any worse. It's not like him to act like this. He never stole a dime from me, not even in his shooting-up days. It was more his style to borrow, then forget to pay back."

I took out a legal pad and wrote down a couple of things. "Okay, but I need you to understand how I work. If I agree to take this case, I can't give you an estimate of how much it's gonna cost you. It's not as simple as taking your car to a mechanic. There's no way I can know in advance how hard it's gonna be to find André, though I'll try to keep the expenses down as much as I can."

"That sounds fair to me."

"I charge a hundred and fifty dollars a day, plus expenses, of course. I usually ask for a deposit up front, to give me some operating cash. If I do the work before I've used up the deposit, I'll return the rest to you. To tell you the truth, I hate to charge you at all, but it's my only business, so I've got to."

He nodded. "It's okay. Really. I've got a little inheritance from an uncle tucked away. It helps support my music career from time to time. I don't see any reason why I can't use some of the money to help my friend. He'd do it for me if the shoe was on the other foot."

"Okay," I said. "I'll need names of other friends of André's, and any relatives. I'll need to talk to his sister and the husband, as well. What's his name, by the way?"

"Carl Pinkham."

West took out a little notebook from his back pocket. "I thought you might need names and addresses, so I brought a few with me. Most of the people on my list are in the Lewiston/Auburn area, but Lucie could give you the names of other relatives scattered around the state, I would think."

I was curious about something. "What about his wife? You haven't mentioned her but once. She must be plenty worried herself by now."

He drummed his fingers on the desk for a moment before answering. "To tell you the truth, I don't know Irene all that well."

I looked at him. "What do you mean? If you were around André that much, certainly you stopped over at the house, or she came to gigs. I don't get it."

"Yeah, well, I don't mean that she hasn't been around or that we didn't talk to each other. It's just that we never got to be buddies or anything. I think she was challenged by all the years André and I have been friends."

"What is she, a jealous newlywed or something?"

He shook his head. "They've been married a few years. But it's as if she has her world and he has his. I've never been able to crack the code and have a real one-on-one conversation with her. Maybe it's just chemistry, I don't know."

I closed up his notebook and handed it back. Then I pulled one of my standard contracts out of a desk drawer. We both signed it and Ernie wrote me a check. We shook hands.

I looked at my watch. "I've just got a couple of things to finish up this morning, then I should be free for the rest of the day. I'll get started by early afternoon. The faster I get to work, the faster we get André home."

I saw what I took to be a flash of relief pass over West's handsome face. "Maybe you'll be able to get some rest now," I said. "These things aren't always as serious as they seem. At any rate, I can take over the reins for a while. You've done what you can do. I'll report anything significant back to you. It's as simple as that."

I sat there for a few minutes after West left, my chair turned around toward the window facing the street, feet propped up on the windowsill, eyes closed. There was no other feeling on earth like the start of a new case, one in which I had a special interest. My blood was humming, revved up like an eight-cylinder '57 Chevy in mint condition, ready to rock and roll.

The transition was over now, and it was André Ledoux, a virtual stranger, who, through his music, had given me a safety valve for the release of emotions I had heaped up in the last few months. His playing had been a simple gift, there for the taking, and I had been in dire need. On some level, I felt as if I owed him, and I believe in paying my debts.

———————

Lucie Pinkham lived in a small white bungalow in Lewiston, on a side street, with window boxes full of petunias and pansies along the front of the house. There was a bit of a porch, also full of flowers—impatiens and marigolds, and some purple flowers I couldn't identify. A healthy-looking ivy plant hung high from a hook to the left of the front door. Someday I was going to have a green thumb, too, I thought.

The trip to Lewiston had taken me a couple of hours, and the day had been perfect for a long ride. The sky was a bright blue, with the occasional puffy cumulus cloud to offset the brilliance. It was summer in Maine, and we who stick around for the long winters have a special appreciation for its warmth and beauty. A blue jay screeching happily from the branches of a chestnut tree in Lucie's yard seemed to agree with my assessment of the day.

I knocked on the front door and waited a few moments while someone turned down the volume on the TV. Then the door swung open and a pretty brunette in her mid-thirties

14

smiled at me questioningly. Piercing brown eyes looked out of an intelligent face; the combination of her prominent Bourbon nose and a high forehead ending in a widow's peak added to her good looks. She was dressed simply, for the heat, in a blue cotton skirt and blouse and sandals. Her medium-length wavy hair was swept back away from her face in a practical-looking cut. She looked like a female version of André Ledoux, minus the hard-living lines etched on his face.

"Lucie Pinkham?" I stuck out my hand. "I'm Lil Ritchie, a private detective hired by Ernie West to locate your brother. I wonder if I might take up a few minutes of your time."

She shook my hand, but surprise flitted across her face. "I didn't know Ernie had done that yet. We'd spoken about it, of course, but I'd hate to cause a fuss if André's just off somewhere by himself."

"Well, I can see your point, but if your brother's in some kind of difficulty, the time element could matter a lot." I looked hopefully past her, into the house. "Do you think we could talk inside?"

Embarrassed, she stepped away from the door and motioned me inside. "Sorry about my manners, Ms. Ritchie—is that your name?" I flashed her my identification, which she gave a brief glance. "I've been worried sick about my brother, and I'm afraid I'm not thinking all that well."

She showed me into the living room, just to the left of the entrance hall. The room was as neat as a pin, just shy of fussy. The furniture was polished to a shine, and needlework doilies were draped over the arms of an easy chair and the sofa. Family photos were lined up on the top of an old spinet piano in the corner and I noticed that sheet music was open on the music stand. It appeared that André Ledoux wasn't the only musician in his family. I sat down on the sofa, while the woman perched tensely on the edge of a straight chair to my right. I glanced over at the TV, which was still on, with the volume turned almost all the way off. The sign of an addict, I thought. " 'Another World' ", I said, "the best soap on TV. I've been watching it for years, on and off, myself."

Lucie smiled. "I always think I'll give it up, but then they start a new story line with Rachel or Cass, and before I know it, I'm hooked again."

"Just like a fish on its way to the frying pan," I said. "I know the intention very well. I grew up in a home where soaps were the highlight of the day. My grandmother once sent a get-well card to Pa on 'As the World Turns' when he was supposedly in the hospital."

"She sent a card to the actor?"

I shook my head. "No. I wish. She sent it to the character he played. I was little, and I remember my mother and an aunt teasing her about it and my grandmother telling them to go straight to hell." I leaned forward. "And she was a Baptist who didn't believe in swearing."

"Thank God I'm not that bad—at least not yet," she said, smiling. Then she settled into the chair and smoothed down her well-ironed skirt. I noticed that she had hardworking hands. "So tell me, Ms. Ritchie, what can I do to help you find André? I probably know him better than anyone else in the world. He's the only brother I have."

I took out my notebook. "First of all, what do you know about the events leading up to his disappearance?"

"Well, I know he was playing somewhere in Augusta and that something went wrong all of a sudden. Ernie told me about it, and I also heard it from Al Sandberg, the drummer. Those three went back a long ways with one another—since school, in fact."

"And you don't have any more idea as to what happened than the others?"

She shook her head. "I wish I did. After that, André was drinking and doing God knows what, and I couldn't get hold of him to make him talk to me. Usually, he will."

16

I nodded. "Now tell me about his coming over here and taking your husband's money."

She looked down at the floor, shame and something else I couldn't identify passing across her face. "I'm sure he didn't mean to do it. He couldn't have been thinking right, to have done that to us."

"But you're sure it was André?"

"I hate to admit it, but it had to be him. He has a key I gave him a while back. Every now and then, he'll use it to let himself in for one thing or another, though mostly it's for sleeping on the sofa after he's played late somewhere. Sometimes he doesn't like to wake up Irene."

I frowned. "How far do he and Irene live from here?"

"Not too far. About ten minutes away."

"I don't get it. What man would sleep on his sister's couch when his own home is nearby? Don't he and his wife get along?"

Again, her face clouded over, and I sensed her struggling with conflicting emotions. "Sometimes they do and sometimes they don't, Ms. Ritchie. It's as plain as that. My brother hasn't always had a very happy life. I'm sure Ernie has told you that. He's had drug and alcohol problems ever since he was a teenager, and I'm afraid it's affected his judgment at times. Irene's not an easy woman to know, so I can't pretend to have her side of all this, but I've never thought she was very good to my brother. Sometimes I think it was just easier for him to come here than to go home."

"It seems to me that you've been a good sister, better than most. Which makes it all the more bizarre that he would steal from you. Has he ever done anything like this before?"

She shook her head emphatically. "No! Not one time has he brought his troubles into this home, not like this. We've lent him money before, and sometimes he's paid it back and at other times he just couldn't. But I've always believed in my brother, and my husband has supported me in this—until now."

I shifted on the sofa and glanced over at the soap opera for a second or two. Sam and Amanda looked as if they'd be hitting the sack any minute now. I looked away, directly into Lucie's troubled eyes. "Is your husband blaming you for this? I see how that might easily happen."

She looked down at her hands, which were again busily smoothing down her skirt. "I guess he does, at that. He's mad as a snake at André, and he even wanted to call the police, but I talked him out of it . . . for now." Tears formed in the corners of her eyes. "I don't know what this is going to do to our marriage, to tell you the truth. I'm torn between my brother and my husband, and that's not a good place to be. Every man likes to feel that he comes first with his wife, you know."

I nodded. "What exactly happened with the theft? I gather you weren't at home."

"I work three days a week at McDonald's. It's a way to get a little extra into the house. I was at work, and when I got home, nothing seemed any different until I walked past the hall closet. The door was open and stuff was thrown around inside."

"Did you think of the money right away?"

"At first, it just seemed so strange, I couldn't seem to grasp what had happened. Then I thought of the lockbox on the top shelf of the closet, and when I saw it had been broken into, I started crying. I called my husband and he came right home from work. I've never seen him so mad." She shivered though it was hot for June.

"And did you both suspect André at first, even though he hadn't done anything like it before?"

"Well, Carl's got a hot temper and sometimes he can jump to conclusions, but I was sure he was wrong . . . he had to be. Then Carl and I went next door to our neighbor Mrs.

18

Kelly, and she said she'd seen André letting himself in with his key in the early afternoon. She's elderly and she sits at her window most all day, watching what she calls her 'stories' and keeping an eye on the comings and goings in the neighborhood. She swears she didn't see anyone but André come in here all day."

I nodded. "I'll speak to her myself, just to see if I can help her remember any other details. I'll also have to talk to your husband, of course."

"I really wish you wouldn't have to talk to Carl. He's upset enough as it is." She looked at me with pleading eyes.

"I understand that. I'll try to be brief, but I have to speak with him. I'll need the name and address of his place of work. Also, I'd like any other names you could give me that might help me find André's whereabouts. Do you have any relatives you think he might turn to?"

She thought for a moment. "I could give you names of our old aunts, but they're kinda spread out all over the state. Some of them live over the border, in Québec. We've stayed in touch with some more than others."

"Well, just in case, you may as well give me their particulars. And if anything else comes up, give me a call." I handed her one of my cards. "Is there anything else you'd like to tell me before I go?"

She didn't look up right away but stopped copying from the address book she'd taken from a side table. "No, I guess not. You've pretty much gotten the gist of it, I think. I just hope you find my brother before Carl gets any madder."

I hoped so, too. I didn't like the look I'd seen cross over Lucie Pinkham's pretty face.

# CHAPTER THREE

# M rs.

Kelly, the next-door neighbor, was a story from another book entirely, something old, maybe even a classic. Frail, birdlike, and lonesome, she ushered me into her house like an overeager child would a potential playmate. She insisted on showing me around the cluttered rooms with obvious pride, and I made the oohing and ahhing sounds that I knew would please her. Her long-dead husband smiled out at us from a World War II photograph, the only one in which, I noticed, he was smiling. "He was a good man, dear, the best there was. We loved each other like there was no tomorrow, I'll tell ya. And when he died from the sugar, I like to have died with 'im." Her fading blue eyes burned into me, and I somehow had no trouble believing what she said.

Satisfied that she had my attention, she headed toward the kitchen and motioned for me to follow. "I'll just get us some lemonade and a cookie or two. I made some peanut-butter cookies yesterday afternoon. I don't know why. But now I have company," she chirped happily.

While she busied herself pouring the lemonade and piling cookies on a plate, I took the opportunity to look her over more carefully. Mrs. Kelly's skin had the translucent quality I'd seen before in the very elderly and her movements, while still fairly quick, were a little on the careful side. Someone who lives alone and is scared of falling, I thought. She wore a flowered green housedress with a thick gray sweater on top, in spite of the afternoon heat.

"There!" She gestured toward the full tray of goodies. "I'll just get you to carry this out to the parlor, if you would. I'm afraid my arthritis won't allow me to pick up anything heavy at all."

Once in her parlor, I settled into a wooden rocker, while she sank into an overstuffed easy chair near the window facing the street. We passed the next few minutes comfortably as she charmed me with stories of her family, living and dead, bits of oral history carried like precious jewels inside her and every other old person. The lemonade was sweet and cold and the cookies were some of the best I'd had in a long time. It took me a while to steer the conversation around to the matter at hand.

"Mrs. Kelly, Lucie Pinkham tells me that you saw her brother, André, letting himself into her house the other day."

She shook her head sadly. "Oh, I'm afraid I did. I wish I hadn't. Poor man, I don't want to cause him any trouble, but I saw him just as clearly as I'm seeing you right now."

I nodded. "Was there anything unusual that you remember from that day? Anything that seemed a little strange at the time, perhaps?"

She thought for a while, frowning in concentration, then shook her head. "No, not really. I wouldn't have thought a thing about it if Lucie and Carl hadn't come over here all upset later in the day."

I decided to try a different tack. "Mrs. Kelly, would you do me a favor and try to think back for a moment? Could you try to remember any sounds you might have heard or any body movements of André's that seemed a little different from the usual ones? Anything at all. It could be very important."

The old woman closed her eyes for a few seconds, and I observed her closely while sipping the lemonade. She had

21

probably told Lucie everything she knew, but our memories can become prematurely fixed sometimes, and I had to make sure there was nothing Mrs. Kelly had forgotten.

When she opened her eyes, I smiled at her hopefully. She shook her head. "I'm afraid I can't remember anything else, Miss Ritchie. I was watching my stories right here in this very chair—it was 'The Young and the Restless', and I'm sure of that, because Nikki was giving Jack a hard time that day because of her drinking, don't you know. Then I looked out the window because I heard a car noise outside."

For a second or two she looked startled, then the look was replaced with one of satisfaction. "You know, I do remember something, now that I think about it. I was surprised to see André's car, because he'd squealed the tires. It sounded like a teenager had pulled up."

"So he'd been speeding? Was it like that?"

She nodded. "Yes. And that wasn't much like him. Sometimes he showed up quite late in the night, you know, and I'd usually not hear him at all. He's a very polite man. I guess I should have noticed that before." Worry began to cloud her face.

"Not at all, Mrs. Kelly. There was no reason you should've remembered that, especially if no one asked you. Let me run this by you, now that you've remembered he arrived in a hurry. Did he get out of the car fast or slowly? Did he take his time going into the house, or did he rush?"

Again, she took her time as she tried to remember. "Well, now that you mention it, he did seem to be in a bit of a hurry. He usually waves hello to me—he knows I'm sitting here a lot—and he most always calls out to the cat that stays under their porch. Poor little thing's afraid of all the dogs around here. And that day, he didn't look left nor right, just used his key and went on inside the house."

It wasn't much, but it was something. I tried to jog the

old woman's memory a little more, but she'd already told me what she knew. I looked at my watch. If I hurried, I could catch Carl Pinkham before he left work.

I left with an invitation to visit, a warm pat on the shoulder, and a Ziploc Baggie chockful of peanut-butter cookies. As I started up the Subaru, something made me look toward the house. Mrs. Kelly stood framed in her doorway, smiling and waving good-bye to me, her new friend. I resisted an old teenager's urge to do a wheelie for her entertainment as I pulled out into traffic.

---

I know that Lewiston and Auburn are separate towns, but to a nonnative, that's a moot point. Like an old married couple, the towns are hopelessly joined, for better or for worse, by the Androscoggin River and a long history, where necessity rules out choice. Trying to locate the muffler shop where I'd find Carl Pinkham, I snaked in and out of Auburn three times before I finally hit on it—Liberty Mufflers, on a busy strip at an edge of town that was part country, part auto graveyard. I sat in the car for a few minutes, watching two mechanics at their work. One of them was removing a muffler with ease from a late-model Ford, while the other wrestled irritably with a rusted-out old clunker. When the muffler finally came off in two pieces and clattered to the floor, the second mechanic looked at it in disgust, shook his head, and pulled out a green bandana to mop the sweat streaming down his face. I got out of the car and headed over to the men.

The sweaty mechanic nodded to me when he noticed my presence. "Can't help you today. We close in ten minutes, but if you bring it back tomorrow, early, we'll try to fit you in." The name embroidered on his shirt was Pinkham.

"Actually, I'd just like to ask you a few questions, Mr. Pinkham. I'm trying to locate your brother-in-law."

For the second time in a few minutes, Carl Pinkham

shook his head. "Shee-it," he said, "I'd like to find him myself, except that he might not like that too much." He smiled grimly.

"Can you talk here, or would you rather go someplace with more privacy?" I eyed the other mechanic, who seemed to find our conversation interesting.

Pinkham put down his wrench and gave me a leer. "You asking me for a date or something?"

"Not hardly," I replied. "But I'll buy you a cold beer if you'll tell me what you know about André Ledoux's disappearance."

He went back to the clunker, turning his back to me in the process. "I don't know a friggin' thing about his so-called disappearance, if that's what you're calling it. He's just run off is all, like the goddamned coward he is."

"Then tell me all about it, at the place of your choosing. It won't take you long, and maybe it'll help locate him sooner."

Pinkham didn't say anything for a minute or two, and I stood there and watched him work. He used his tools skillfully and with care, even though this seemed like the end of a long day. He was small and wiry but muscular, with a thin, oval face. A blue gimme cap covered most of his brown hair and he wore it turned up slightly. He turned toward me and his small brown eyes registered surprise that I was still standing there. He obviously didn't know enough about stubborn Southern women.

"C'mon," I said. "One beer won't kill you. Then you'll be rid of me and you can go home, put your feet up, and catch Tom Brokaw."

He grunted once, then finally sighed. "Okay. The Twilight Lounge, then. Two miles up, on the right, toward town. And you're paying. I'll be there in a couple of minutes."

The Twilight Lounge didn't look like my kind of bar. Set just far enough off the busy road to leave room for three or

24

four parking spaces in front, it abutted a potholed lot off to one side. Pickups littered the property like a herd of dust-drenched, tired cattle. The bar's nearest neighbors were an auto-parts store, a machine shop, and a liquor store, where business seemed to be booming. Across the road, I noticed a small factory whose name gave no information as to what might be produced inside. Men carrying lunch boxes now poured out of it as if the place was about to blow up.

When I walked into the bar, I understood why they'd named it the Twilight. A few heads turned in my direction, but no one seemed more interested in me than in their beers. I didn't take it personally. It had been a scorcher and Mainers weren't all that used to the heat. I took a seat at the bar and ordered a Bud.

A couple of minutes later, Carl Pinkham slid onto the stool next to me. "How'd you know I watch Brokaw?" he asked by way of a greeting. "Is my whole friggin' life written all over me or something?"

I shook my head. "Just a lucky guess. You look like a shortstop, and he's a baseball man."

He gave me a semblance of a grin, then ordered a small pitcher. He lit up a Marlboro and blew out a lungful of smoke before speaking again. "So how come you're lookin' for André? He rip you off, too?"

"Nope. I'm a detective, hired by Ernie West. He was the one who told me about the theft. Today, I interviewed your wife, and I'm trying to talk to anyone else with any information I can go on."

He drank his first beer down in three swallows and started pouring another. "Shee-it, it's hot. I hate this heat, man. Used to be, there were only two weeks of hot weather in the summer, but now we're just like the rest of the stinkin' country."

I'd heard this before from other natives and pretty much believed it. The greenhouse effect, most likely.

"So why do you think André stole your money?"

Pinkham shrugged. "Why does a dog bark? I figure it this way—he gets back on the dope and the sauce and needs to pay some dealer off or somethin'. We were the easiest way to get the money probably."

I asked him something I'd been wondering about all day. "How come you kept that much money in the house? Haven't you heard of banks?"

He flashed me a dirty look and stubbed his cigarette out angrily in the ashtray. "It was stupid as shit, I guess. But sometimes I moonlight a little at night, tune-ups and oil changes and minor repairs, mostly around the neighborhood. Uncle Sam gets enough of my money as it is. I figured it was a way to keep a little bit saved back in case something happened."

I made a mental note to check that out later.

"The wrong something happened, didn't it? You sure you didn't run him out of town yourself?"

He slammed his mug down, and I felt the whole bar staring at us. "Who the hell do you think you are? I don't know you, lady, and you sure as hell don't know me," he said angrily. "I opened our house up to that fucker and look what he did. You're damned right I'm pissed."

I ran with it. "But you don't know what happened to him? You'll swear to it?"

"I ain't swearing to nothin'. I see him, his ass is grass, but I guess he already knows that. It'll take him a while to show his face, I s'pose."

"And then what will you do?"

He shook his head, then finished his beer and stood up to leave. "You'll just have to wait to find out, won't you?"

I didn't like the sounds of that. "You do something to André and you'll break your wife's heart. You'd do well to keep that in mind."

He lowered his voice and stepped close enough for me to

smell his sweat, the beer and cigarettes on his breath, and his anger. "That's my wife and my house. That makes it my business. You get that? Don't mess with me, lady. You wouldn't like it much."

He was more right than he knew. He slammed the front door going out and the bartender frowned at me hostilely. I suppose this is Carl Pinkham's bar, too, I thought. At any rate, it was beginning to feel like leaving time. I tossed some bills down on the bar but took my time walking out, in imitation of Littlefield, who always keeps his dignity.

The bartender neglected to say, "Come again." Maybe he just forgot.

# CHAPTER FOUR

There
was one more person I needed to talk with before I could
return home to Tillman for the night. Irene Ledoux had so
far been nothing but a bit player in her husband's drama, and
no one I'd spoken to had thought this odd. But something
about her noninvolvement didn't quite fit and so I decided
not to leave town without getting some sort of fix on her.

I wandered around the limboland of Lewiston/Auburn,
hopelessly lost, until I chanced upon a sign for Bates College.
Pulling over, I studied the map once more and realized where
I'd been making my mistake. I turned around and headed
back into working-class Lewiston. Five minutes later, I pulled
up in front of André and Irene Ledoux's house.

The neighborhood was similar to Lucie and Carl's, with
mostly small, solidly built one-story wood bungalows erected
between the two World Wars. They all had a porch, a yard,
and a few fair-sized trees. I thought of the pride of the first
families of factory workers to move into these shining new
homes as they got their first shot at the American dream. For
a few minutes, I sat in the Subaru, quietly taking in the feel
of the street, listening to the barking dogs, the chirping birds,
and the happy voices of children at play. I saw a brother and
sister racing on bikes in response to their mother's call to
supper. The boy won by a hair, but both children laughed as
they ran inside. The perfection of the scene was marred by my

suddenly remembering that the man who lived in the house I was preparing to enter was a world-class musician who had squandered much of his life as a junkie and a drunk. Just why he had recently chosen to move back to his hometown was a missing piece I still needed to find if I was going to make sense of the puzzle of his life and bring him home once more.

As I rapped on the door, I heard music inside. No one answered at first, so I amused myself playing a game of Name That Tune. Whatever it was, it sounded sweet—too sweet for my taste—and was hardly what I expected from a jazzman's wife. I knocked again, this time a little louder, and after another, shorter wait, I saw a face behind the thin curtain covering the glassed top half of the door. I flashed my ID, and the woman inside tentatively cracked the door a few inches.

Suspicious brown eyes took me in from head to foot. I sucked in my gut and forced a smile.

"Ms. Ledoux, I'm looking for your husband and I need to ask you a few questions, if you don't mind."

She frowned. "Looking for my husband? Who hired you?"

"Ernie West," I said.

She shook her head and smiled a bitter smile. "I shoulda known. Tweedledum and Tweedledee."

I let that comment pass while she decided whether to talk to me or run me off her porch. Irene Ledoux wasn't what I'd expected, although five minutes before, I wouldn't have said I'd been expecting any particular type of person. She was sturdily built, tending toward stockiness, with blondish brown hair that had been permed recently and possibly dyed. Lines deeply etched around her eyes and mouth indicated some hard knocks, taken or given. She'd poured herself into a pair of red pants that appeared to be made from a miracle fabric, completing her outfit with a green-and-white horizontally striped top. Her lipstick was an unfortunate shade of pink that did little to pull her color scheme together.

In the few seconds it took me to register these observations, her eyes never once left my face.

"Suit yourself," she said gracelessly, "but he'll be back. Just like a cat." She opened the door and stepped aside for me to enter.

The air inside the house was stale. Cooking odors lingered, mixed unpleasantly with a cloying room-deodorizer scent. Irene Ledoux stepped around me and led the way into the living room.

"Have a seat," she said. "I'll just go turn down my music."

While I perched uncomfortably on the edge of a sofa covered in clear plastic, I realized with a start that the music I'd heard from the porch was so-called Christian light rock. The musicians played a basic rock beat and basic rock chords, but with all the passion removed. A male singer droned on about God knows what, giving John Lennon a turn in his grave, I was sure. Holy shit, I thought, no wonder André Ledoux sleeps on his sister's couch.

"Nice music," I lied when Irene returned. "Is this a local station?" I smiled my most ingratiating smile.

She dropped heavily into a recliner across the room from me and pressed down a lever that made the chair tilt back.

"It's from Portland," she said. "Now, what can I do for you?"

Okay, I thought, if we're gonna be all business, let's get down. "Ms. Ledoux, where do you think your husband is?"

She shrugged. "Beats me. I assume he's off somewhere by himself."

"Aren't you worried? I understand that when André took off, you called Ernie West in a panic."

"Yeah, well maybe I did, but I've had some time to think it over by now. This isn't the first time my husband's taken off and it won't be the last. It's just something he does from time to time."

30

"What would you say triggers it?"

She shrugged again. "Pressure mostly. Things get tight, André splits. He's been doing it for as long as I've known him, and a lot longer than that."

I decided to try another tack. "How long have you and André been married?"

"Three years, off and on. We separated a couple of times. Do I have to take time off for the times we were apart, or does it still count?" She smiled, but her eyes kept up their steady surveillance.

It was my turn to shrug. "If it counts with you, it counts with me. So would you say your marriage is a happy one?"

"What does that have to do with anything? I'm a Christian woman and I don't believe in divorce. My husband is the one I've got and I'm not one to let go."

Somehow I believed her, as far as it went. I asked her something I'd been wondering about for a while. "What caused you to move here to Maine? Weren't you living somewhere out West?"

She reached for a cigarette, a menthol by the smell of it. "We've lived from pillar to post, you might say. Suddenly, before Christmas, André got a bee in his bonnet to come home to Maine, and no amount of talking could keep him from getting his way. So that's what we did."

"And how has it been, being here on his home turf, Ms. Ledoux? Some wives would like it, some not, I'd suppose."

She blew out a thick blue stream of smoke. "I didn't want to do it at first, but now I'm kinda glad I did. Here, he's busy with his music and I've got my church, so it works out okay."

I pretended to write something down in my little notebook while I decided how to phrase my next question.

"Has religion always been such a big part of your life, then? Forgive me for asking, but jazz music and religion haven't necessarily always gone hand in hand."

"Well, maybe they should've. I'm born-again and it's

turned my whole life around. I only wish everybody could feel what I do." She locked her eyes with mine and I squirmed on the hot couch. I knew what was coming.

"And what about you? Have you felt the love of Jesus Christ our Savior?"

The hell with it, I thought. I'd had enough of Bible bullies, growing up in the South. "I have my beliefs, Ms. Ledoux, which give me comfort. I do okay with them."

She smiled slightly. "That's what I thought," she said.

I fought down a smoldering anger. It wasn't the beliefs that got to me, it was the smugness that accompanied them. And as for André Ledoux, troubled, sensitive genius, I just couldn't picture him in this overwhelming, stifling atmosphere.

I took a deep breath.

"Ms. Ledoux, what can you tell me about André's latest troubles?"

She sat up in her recliner and ground out her cigarette in the ashtray next to it. "There's not much to tell. He went to play in Augusta and didn't come home when he was supposed to. When he did, he was in bad shape, with drink on his breath."

"Didn't this alarm you?" I asked.

She shook her head. "I've seen this many, many times. More than anyone knows. My husband's got a self-destructive side like you wouldn't believe. Things go too smooth, and next thing you know, I'm picking him up in the drunk tank."

I frowned. "But I thought he'd been in good shape for a while and had licked his problems to some extent."

She gave a half-smile, then started pulling at a hangnail that was apparently troubling her. "People don't know him the way I do," she said. "His friends and family see what they want to see, but I know better."

*Smug* was starting to seem like an understatement. I decided to rattle her cage and see what would happen.

"What do you know about your husband's theft of one thousand dollars from his sister and her husband?"

This time, I'd thrown the woman. Her veneer of control fell like a soufflé taken out of the oven too soon. Ha! I thought nastily. That wasn't so hard, was it?

"What thousand dollars?" she said. "I didn't know anything about this. Why hasn't someone told me? When did this happen?"

For a moment, I watched the woman's agitation, then decided it looked real enough. Okay, I said to myself, fair is fair. "He stole the money on his way out of town, it seems. At least that's what it looks like as of now. I'd like to find him before Carl Pinkham decides to press charges and makes André's position worse."

She reached for another cigarette, then stopped herself. "Well, it's beyond me," she said. "I was beginning to think my husband couldn't surprise me, but I guess I was wrong."

I nodded. I had run out of questions for the time being.

I stood up, and Irene, with a look of relief on her face, jumped to her feet. "Thanks, Ms. Ledoux. You've been very helpful."

She looked at her watch. "I'd better go myself, or the prayer meeting will have to start without me."

I handed her one of my business cards. "I'd appreciate it if you would call me if you think of anything else that might help me locate André."

"I'll do that," she said, although I wasn't at all sure she'd do anything of the sort.

The woman was a hard one to get a handle on.

I walked slowly to the car and sat inside the Subaru for a few minutes, with the radio tuned to a Portland rock station. I needed to purge my head of the syrupy Christian Muzak I'd been force-fed inside the Ledoux house. Then I heard the unmistakable opening chords of "People Are Strange," and

Jim Morrison, dead for as many years as he'd lived, crooned away my black mood.

———————

On the way out of town, I decided to drive past the huge Gothic cathedral I'd noticed towering over the city. I passed empty-looking factories, their windows boarded up, the occupants long gone. Modern buildings downtown stood in the shadows of failed businesses that seemed to send dire warnings from the past. I wondered what it was like to have grown up and lived in the midst of all that apparent failure.

Perched on one of the highest hills in town, the granite cathedral was even larger than I expected. It took up a full city block. I love anything with a tower, and this place had towers galore. Despite its size, there was an airy grace to the huge church, due perhaps to its unusual blend of Art Deco and Norman architecture. Scaffolding clung to the front of it, but there were no workmen in sight.

I got out of the car and walked up the front steps, craning my neck to see details of the bell-tower faces. I tried the front door and got nowhere, then walked around to the back. At a side entrance, I was able to get inside, but all the doors leading into the church proper were locked. Great, I thought. Finally, you try to go to church and you can't even get in. I dawdled in front of an information table, picked up a couple of pamphlets, and was preparing to leave, when an inner door opened.

The priest was somewhere in his sixties, short and roly-poly, with a curious smile on his face. "I'm sorry," he said now. "I didn't mean to startle you, but I hadn't heard you come in."

I smiled back. "I was just driving by and became interested in what the inside of your church looked like. I guess I'm sort of trespassing, but it's not intentional. I can come back some other time."

"Not at all. I would be glad to give you a tour, but I'm

on my way to visit one of our parishioners in the hospital. She's an elderly person who just broke her hip."

I nodded. "That's tough, all right. She must be pretty upset."

"She's afraid her family will send her to a nursing home. That's one of the fears that goes along with broken hips and the elderly."

"I hope she'll pull through okay." I turned around and put my hand on the door. "I'm curious about one thing. How did it happen that something this magnificent was built here in Lewiston? The scale of it seems a little out of the ordinary to me."

The priest rattled around some change in his pants pocket. "It was built with money from the mill workers around the turn of the century. They imported the granite from North Jay, Vermont. They were French-Canadians who had come down earlier looking for work and settled around the mill towns. I say 'they,' although that's also my own background. Then, when most of the textile mills moved south after World War Two, some of the workers were forced to go down to Massachusetts and Connecticut, but others stayed right here."

"There's still a big Franco-American population, then?"

He nodded. "Oh yes. We're a gentle people, very family-oriented, and we work hard. We prefer to stay close to home, *chez nous*, whenever possible." His eyes twinkled mischievously, challenging me to remember my high school French.

*"Chez nous*—'at home,' " I said. *"C'est exact?"*

The priest laughed. "You're not bad, mademoiselle. All you need is a little practice. Yes, that's right. Many of us have relatives on both sides of the border even today. Lewiston is still an important center for our culture. Leaving it would break a link."

I could see his point. "And you? Were you born here?"

He shook his head. "No, madame, I was born near Rivière-du-Loup, Québec. I was one of fourteen children—just six years old when my parents came down here to work in the mills. So this is home to me, but not totally. Each year I go up to Québec and almost every year someone from my family comes down here to see me. I live in two cultures. Many of us here do."

"And some people can't even remember if they have *one*," I muttered.

The priest laughed again. He seemed a happy man. "Well, yes, the modern times have led some of us a little astray, haven't they?" He looked at me with his pretty blues and I could feel him become interested in my reason for being in town. "So what brings you here, mademoiselle? If I may ask, did you come to Lewiston to visit someone?"

I made a quick decision. "Well, I guess you could say that. I'm a private detective and I'm looking for someone who lives here. I've interviewed everyone I'm going to today, but I suppose I'm looking for a bigger context to fit everything into. I just stumbled in here, the way I stumble into other places. It felt right."

He frowned. "And might I ask who you're searching for?"

"André Ledoux," I said. "He grew up around here and recently moved back to Maine."

The priest raised his bushy eyebrows and nodded solemnly. "André Ledoux. I'd wondered what had happened to him in recent years. I'd heard about his success in music, but also the rumors about drugs and so forth."

A light bulb went on in my head. "So you knew him? When was that?"

He shrugged. "A long time ago, when he was just a child. Little André and his sister were from this neighborhood. He was an altar boy for a time. He was such a sweet, gentle boy—not like some of the ruffians you see now, and not even like me and my brothers." He smiled. "We were a rough-and-tumble lot. But this André, he had something special in him. Mind you, he could be as rough as the rest when he played, but then he would immediately turn around and be as kind as could be to the smaller children. He loved his little sister. I can still see him taking her hand to cross the street. I was sad to hear of his other problems. Maybe we didn't make him strong enough, after all."

"Can you remember any things about him that might help me understand the man? I want to find him before he gets into more trouble than he's already in with his family."

He thought a minute, staring at the floor tiles in concentration. "He and his sister—Lucie, that would be—lost their father in an alcohol-related accident when they were just teenagers. He was a hardworking man—oh, how that man worked to raise his family. But his fondness for whiskey got the better of him. Their mother, what a lovely woman she was. She died of cancer a few years back. She loved to laugh and she loved to sing—I can hear her now." He closed his eyes and rocked back on his heels, listening. "That's probably where André got his talent. The children hadn't quite finished growing up when their father was killed, but they did the best they could, as did their mother. She was a beautiful seamstress and she supported herself and the children that way, doing her best. Lucie still comes to Mass, but I haven't discussed that period of her life with her in a long time. She's a fine young woman, and I would suspect that André is a fine man, at least in his heart."

I smiled at the priest. "I believe you're right about André. And he's as talented a man as we're likely to see on this earth."

"If you need my help, will you come to me?" The priest looked concerned. "I don't know what I can do, but I'm willing." He held out his hand. "I'm Father Jean-Pierre Larose, by the way. Now I must go or an old woman's cursing will be on my conscience."

His hand was cool and steady and he smiled courteously. "You've already helped me, Father, but if I think of anything else, I'll be in touch. And good luck." We walked out of the church together.

I drove back to Tillman in a quiet mood, with André Ledoux's haunting guitar more than filling the Subaru. His latest release was one of his best, both dynamic and gentle, his playing often sounding like the work of two guitarists instead of one. A combination of old standards and original compositions, his music stretched across several styles and built bridges where none had been. Yet one could also detect pain and grief, and a hint of despair.

When he'd picked me to find his friend, Ernie West had made a good choice. I cared for the man, I loved his music, and now I had a broader sense of who he was. I would find him. I'd have a good night's sleep, a cuddle with Littlefield, and then I'd burn up the highways, if that was what it would take to bring him back home.

# CHAPTER FIVE

I knew I was in trouble the moment I pulled into my yard. I sat motionless in the driver's seat, waiting for what was to come, the better to get it over with fast. Sure enough, Littlefield jumped onto the hood of the car with a heavy thud, frowning furiously. I froze as he walked around to the side-view mirror and peered in at me. In one quick movement he was inside the car, yowling and howling his displeasure, stepping all over me, from lap to shoulder, before finally turning around, satisfied, his back parts placed strategically in my face. Dinner was late and I would pay.

"So who signed a contract?" I said defensively. "Who says I've eaten, myself?"

No matter. I knew the routine. I opened the car door and he jumped out and raced for the porch steps, singing off-key while I fumbled around with the lock. He was in before I was, waiting by his dish, switching his tail back and forth.

"Oh, all right, you spoiled little rat with fur, I'll feed ya. What would you like—strychnine, savory stew, or liver and beef?"

You couldn't insult him. He went for the savory stew, his favorite, and made a mess of it. I watched as he finished off the food in his dish and the rest that he'd splattered on the floor nearby. Happy at last, he sashayed over to his cushion by the kitchen table and proceeded to wash himself.

"You cat guys have the good life," I said. "Who's gonna

feed me, the breadwinner of this sorry family?" I opened the fridge and peered inside, praying for leftovers. Sure enough, there was a container of white clam sauce from a couple of nights ago. I drank a little wine while the pasta cooked, then ate just as ravenously as Littlefield when my turn came.

I'd had a long day. I went to bed before midnight, with Laurie Colwin's *Goodbye Without Leaving* for company. Her main character, Geraldine, had been a white backup singer in a soul show, a fantasy I didn't have any trouble plugging into. I'm sure I went to sleep with a smile on my face, although the cat certainly wouldn't be one to tell. Littlefield and I have our secrets.

---

The next morning was another beauty. I sat on my back steps and enjoyed some morning espresso while I planned my day. A light breeze off the water sent the sweet-sour smell of the sea my way, while my neighbor Fred's mock orange competed nicely in the fragrance department. Yellow-and-black butterflies danced gaily around the white blossoms, interrupted only by the busy work of the honeybees. It was one of the days we humans don't have to ask ourselves why we are alive.

I tuned out the morning for a moment or two and thought about the case that would occupy my day. Let's see what we have, I thought. There's Ernie West, who's upset about his missing friend; there's André's sister, Lucie, concerned for her brother and worried about her husband's temper; then there's Carl Pinkham, a hothead of the first order, madder than hell; and last, but not least, Irene Ledoux, the wife—concerned at first but not now—a religious nut who smokes menthols. When I found André Ledoux, I'd get him to explain it all to me.

Meanwhile, I would check the answering machine in my office and run a couple of errands before I questioned anyone else. I threw on an old pair of cutoffs and a T-shirt, remembering to bring along a respectable pair of jeans and a light shirt just in case. Littlefield had his full attention on the dandelion he was stalking and didn't give me so much as a glance when I left.

There weren't any messages on my machine that couldn't wait. Two of them were from the same person, an ex-client who had gotten a little too attached and had mistaken my professional interest for a personal one. He was my mechanic's cousin, and, if worse came to worse, I'd have to set him straight. For now, I would ignore him.

I used the keys Molly had given me and added some mail to the stack in her office. Molly was a lawyer, but, more importantly, an old friend. We worked together sometimes and found it convenient to have offices across a hallway from each other. Just now, she'd taken off abruptly for a couple day's kayaking and camping off the coast on Isle au Haut. It wasn't much like her. I knew she had a heavy caseload, and besides, she hated camping during blackfly season. When she came back, I would grill her mercilessly, but for now, I did what I was told.

Back at my desk, I thumbed through the addresses Ernie West and Lucie Pinkham had given me. Lucie had said that she and André hadn't seen their aunts much in recent years, but I knew that these family connections could be important in times of crisis. I decided against calling, although it would be at least a two-hour drive to the nearest aunt. I grabbed a handful of cassette tapes and took off.

---

Popping Van Morrison's *Hymns to the Silence* into the tape deck, I opened the windows. The air that rushed in was as sweet as a ripe mango. Van still had it.

The ride to Bangor took me an hour. In less traffic, the trip could have taken forty-five minutes—that's summer in vacationland for you. By July, more than a million tourists have already crossed the bridge at the New Hampshire border and headed east and north, a fact many natives accept with divided minds, knowing as they do that money and aggrava-

41

tion often come in the same Winnebagos. I tried to remember enough math to multiply eight hundred miles—the approximate distance to the Midwest—by thirty-five miles an hour and came to my conclusion, a variation on a theme by Thomas Wolfe: They'd never go home again. Not until after leaf season, anyway.

My slow speed had its advantages, though. The great north woods are never far from you in this part of Maine, so I decided to relax and enjoy the scenery. After a few miles, I shifted into third gear to take some steep hills. On either side of the road, all I could see was woods as far as the eye reached: firs, pines, maples, and birch, mixed in with poplars, ash, and beech.

I knew these woods to be full of black bears and white-tailed deer, red foxes, raccoons, fishers, beavers, porcupines, bobcats, and coyotes. Around here, it's also not unusual to spot a moose—as often as not, strolling casually down the white line of the highway. I know people who've encountered a lone black bear or coyote right in town, as well. I like this life in a place where nature hasn't been fully subjugated yet.

Musing along, I slipped onto 395 and circled the twin cities of Brewer and Bangor. I always enjoy the way they hug the river as I cross the new bridge over the Penobscot to points west and north. Today, the river was magnificent, wide at high tide and as deep and powerful as I fancied it to have been in pre-Colonial times. Beyond the downtown waterfront, grand houses still stood on the high bank, left over from the days when lumber barons and sea captains supplied Maine wood to distant ports. Many of the houses were crowned with widow's walks for observing the menfolk as they came home or failed to come home on some unfortunate family's day of dread and sorrow.

I picked up I-95 and headed north, past the turnoff to Orono and the University of Maine campus and then past the exit for Old Town and Indian Island, home of the Penobscot Nation. The trees crowding along the highway now were mostly white pines, the kings of the Pine Tree State. I could feel the stirrings of excitement as the great north woods opened up before me. Soon, the Lagrange exit appeared and I started to snake northwest on Route 16, through a mix of woodlots, fields, and small villages.

A little beyond Lagrange, not far from Milo, I braked to a stop and backed up to a car-and-truck graveyard. Buried in the woods on either side and barely visible from the road were old vehicles from the twenties and thirties—trucks, cars, and at least one bus, all very rusty, many still intact. Trees and bushes had grown around these relics and wildflowers sprouted from front seats and half-open trunks. I got out of the Subaru, took a good stretch, and leaned against the front fender for a few minutes, savoring nature's victory over the mechanized world.

A little before reaching Milo, the road crossed the Piscataquis River, which would empty into the Penobscot farther east. I was entering serious lake country, where hundreds of streams empty into ponds and lakes known to fishermen from many parts of the country. The mountains I was beginning to see on the horizon were the Appalachians, whose northern extremity was in nearby Baxter State Park. I was born and raised near the Blue Ridge in Virginia and have always felt my roots to be solidly connected to the Appalachians. The sight of my mountain chain in such a different setting always throws me off a little, as would the vision of a parent all dressed up and dancing with a stranger.

Soon I entered the little town of Milo, where I took Route 11 toward Brownville. There I gassed up at a friendly Mobil station where the attendant cheerfully gave me directions to Brownville Junction and to André's aunt's house.

Eulalie Tremblay lived on a narrow dirt road that curved upward, toward the mountains, just outside the Junction. I crossed the railroad tracks three times before I saw the small farmhouse set back from the road near a birch wood. I slowed down to a crawl, reading the mailbox to be certain. Its rough lettering told me I was at the home of Jean and Eulalie Tremblay, although no one had mentioned an uncle to me. I turned into the driveway.

I parked near the house, behind an old, well-kept Buick, waiting before I opened the car door to see whether I would be greeted by dogs. When no dogs appeared, I cautiously got out and stretched, looking around. The house was small, the yard well kept, and there were flowers of every possible color in neat beds around the house. Old tires painted white held peonies and petunias. Violets bloomed in window boxes and carefully groomed shrubs stood sentry in front of the porch. The grass had been mown recently and the smell of it still permeated the air. I breathed it in deeply. It was then that I noticed the other car.

Just ahead of the Buick was a little combination garage and woodshed. Parked in it was a blue Toyota. I glanced toward the house, and when no one looked back, I took a casual stroll. The two bumper stickers I saw on the Toyota caused my heart to start racing. The first one said GUITARISTS MAKE THE BEST LOVERS. The second one was the clincher, though: FESTIVAL INTERNATIONAL DE JAZZ DE MONTRÉAL. It was last summer's logo and matched its twin on my Subaru. I'd found André Ledoux.

---

I knocked gingerly on the front door, my heart still pounding. A heavyset elderly woman greeted me as she pushed the screen door outward. She was dressed simply in a shirtwaist with a floral print. The dress appeared to be starched and ironed and the apron she wore on top had nary a stain. Her gray hair was pinned back in a bun that was as tight and solid as the woman herself, if I was any judge of character at all.

I smiled at her now. "Mrs. Tremblay, I'm trying to locate your nephew, André, and couldn't help but notice his car over there." I gestured toward the garage.

44

Her shrewd eyes took me in. She leaned out and peered over at my car. "You say you search for my nephew, but you don't say why. How you t'ink I feel about dat? I don't know you."

Her accent was country French and her words dipped and rose in a lyrical way that was quite unlike the patterns of native English speakers. She was two generations closer to her roots than the current generation of Franco-Americans, and it showed.

"Mrs. Tremblay, I'm a private detective, hired by André's friend Ernie West. I only wish to talk to your nephew to see if I can help him out. I mean no one any harm."

"Ha!" She laughed. "Sometime de people don't mean 'arm, but sometime it come along with de morning itself." She held on to the door, barring my way, an immovable force.

I thought quickly. "What if you just let me talk to André, in front of you? Out here on the porch, even. He knows me a little. He won't think I'm here to hurt him."

"André is not 'ere for talking, I don't t'ink. 'E's sleeping now. 'E's very tired." She pronounced it "tee-red," but I got the message.

"Do you think I could wait out here in my car until he wakes up, then? Mrs. Tremblay, I mean no disrespect, but I'm not leaving here until I've spoken with him. It's my job, and besides, I'm worried about him."

The old woman took a deep breath, puffing herself up to look even bigger. "You want to wait for 'im, den you wait by the road over dere." She pointed toward the highway. "I don't want that you make 'im afraid and unquiet."

I turned away as she went in, prepared to wait by the highway if that was what it would take. I'd come too far to be intimidated by this old woman, although I found myself admiring her earthy methods.

I'd reached the bottom step when the sound of the spring on the screen door made me turn around. André Ledoux stood uncertainly on the porch, looking at me in

45

confusion. He was wearing a white T-shirt and jeans and had a three-day stubble. His hair stood up on end and his eyes were red from lack of sleep or from booze. His aunt stood behind him, her hand on his back, patting and soothing him the way one would comfort a scared child.

I sprang into action before either of them could bolt. "André, you remember me, right? Lil Ritchie. I'm a great fan of yours."

He frowned for a moment, then smiled shyly. "Of course I remember you. I just wasn't planning on seeing you here."

I pushed on. "Do you think we might talk? Ernie has hired me to find you. He thinks you might be in some trouble. I'd like to help if I can."

He thought about it for a few seconds, then spoke quietly in French to his aunt. She nodded and looked me over once again from bottom to top. When she'd finished, she'd made up her mind. "Would you like to 'ave some lunch with us? Dere's plenty for one more."

Her guttural *r* gave the language a completely new feel. As I noted this, I realized that I'd been holding my breath in. I let it out now and said I'd be honored to have lunch with them. I meant it, too. "Den come inside before de bugs get in. I'll set de table." She turned into the kitchen.

We were alone for just a moment and I started to ask André the questions that had been burning inside me. He seemed to sense this and simply said, "We might as well go in. Tante Eulalie will worry otherwise." He held the door open for me and I entered the house.

It was as neat as any I'd ever been in—convent parlor–neat. There were afghans on the sofas, cushions on the chairs, lace doilies carefully placed on arm- and headrests. Every furniture surface was polished to a bright shine. André led me to an immaculate large kitchen where a round table was now set for three. His aunt stood at the stove, cutting wedges from a meat pie that smelled so good, my stomach started growling.

46

I crossed the linoleum floor to stand politely near the table. "Please sit down," she said. "Pour yourself a cup of coffee if you'd like." She gestured toward a dented old percolator-type coffee maker sitting next to a mug full of teaspoons in the middle of the table. Country practicality, I thought—you keep the spoons where they do the most good. André indicated where I should sit and I took my place at the table. In seconds, we had plates of steaming-hot meat pie and mashed potatoes in front of us. I was in heaven. André poured us all cups of coffee. I took mine black. I had a bite of the pie and closed my eyes in appreciation. "What is this?" I said. "It's the best thing I've ever eaten."

Eulalie allowed a small smile to cross her face, which transformed her instantly from a fearsome woman warrior into a beloved elderly aunt. "It's only *tourtière*, mademoiselle, pork pie, I t'ink you say. We French, we like them very much."

André spoke for the first time since entering the kitchen. He cleared his throat and dared to look directly at me, something he'd been avoiding until now. "This is a traditional dish from Québec. It's eaten during *réveillon*, which is the celebration that happens on Christmas Eve, after midnight Mass."

I noticed that the others had put catsup on their pies, so I did the same. "But it's not Christmas," I said, belaboring the obvious.

His aunt spoke up. "At Christmas, you 'ave to eat *tourtière*, but today we eat it just because we like it. Also, not all people go to Mass dese days, Christmas or no." She shot a quick glance at André, who pretended not to notice.

By the second cup of coffee, André had relaxed a little and his aunt was no longer looking at me out of the corner of her eye. "André, can we talk about why you left home so abruptly?" I asked gently. "Ernie and your sister are worried sick and they wanted me to find you."

André tucked his head—in shame, perhaps, or something else—I didn't know him well enough to tell. "I just wanted to be by myself for a few days. I have some things to figure out."

I glanced at his aunt, not wanting to mention the missing cash in front of the old woman. "I believe I might know one or two reasons you wanted to get away, but I don't think anything will be solved by running. Why don't you come back with me? I could help you fix whatever's wrong." I sincerely meant it. This man had had a hard life, and if I could help any part of it flow a little easier, I wouldn't turn my back.

He sighed and pushed away his plate, his food only half-eaten. His aunt gave me a dirty look, then rose to clear away our dishes.

"There are things no one understands about what's happening," he said. "I'm not so sure myself. Maybe I'll be ready to go home soon, but not right now."

I leaned toward him. "Then talk to me, André. Tell me what's going on and we can start from there. I'm a patient woman and I'm a good fixer. Just ask anyone who knows me."

He looked at me long and hard, and I noticed his aunt doing the same from her place in front of the sink. "What is it you need?" I asked. "More time? Because if that's what it is, I could stay somewhere nearby and we could talk. Then, if you're ready to go back tomorrow or the next day, I could go back with you and help protect your interests."

I shut up abruptly, letting my words sink in. André and his aunt exchanged another glance, but it was a private look, a family look, and I didn't have a clue as to its meaning.

Finally, he spoke again, rubbing his eyes, which didn't look any less red for my stimulating company or the delicious meal. "I'm really wiped out, Lil. I can't explain anything until I've rested. I just can't think."

I took the hint. "What if I found a motel room nearby and we got together to talk later in the day, after you've slept? That would be fair, I think. I don't have to be anywhere else for a while." I was banking on his being too exhausted to bolt.

He shook his head and smiled. "You don't give up, do you?"

I smiled back at him. "Not often," I said, "not if it's important to me."

He got up from the table and took his aunt by the arm. "Excuse us for just a moment, will you? My aunt and I need to speak in private." They left the room for a couple of minutes, which I spent counting the cabbage roses on the linoleum.

His aunt entered the room alone. "My nephew 'as gone to sleep, mam'zelle. 'E is very tee-red. It is all right if you wait 'ere, as you please. Den you talk to 'im."

What choice did I have?

Eulalie took off her apron and smoothed down her hair. "I go to the 'ome of my friend Madame D'Amour. We play dominoes t'ree times each week, good weather or bad." She smiled and once again her face was transformed. "You make like at 'ome. I t'ink André, 'e is not going to sleep too long."

I thanked her for her hospitality and silently marveled at her old-timey trust. I was a stranger and in the space of little more than an hour she had given me the free run of her home. She poured me a glass of iced tea before leaving.

I spent much of the afternoon wandering through the house and the yard, enjoying the feel of being in someone else's private space. When I grew tired of this mild form of snooping, I sat down on the porch and thought about André Ledoux and his wonderful gift to the world. Separating the man from the gift was virtually impossible, even though I knew that often the fragile human personality could suffer by comparison.

As late afternoon came, I began to feel restless. Expecting André to sleep a little longer, I grabbed my acoustic guitar out of the backseat of the Subaru. I prefer playing the electric guitar, but six strings beat no strings, and I never know when I might like to play for a few minutes. Private detectives spend a fair amount of time in motels and it's nice to have something other than the all-pervasive tube for entertainment.

I settled down on the porch steps and proceeded to hypnotize myself into a peaceful finger-picking trance. Thoughts of Andre's predicament melted away as I picked my way through a few of my favorite Appalachian tunes: "Gold Watch and Chain," "The Cuckoo," "The River in the Pines," and "Shady Grove." I sang softly, not wanting to wake the tired man whose aura was all around me even as he slept. From there, I switched repertoires and played songs of a more contemporary cast, ending up with a favorite, "Through the Darkness," by Cats on Holiday, a Virginia band I liked:

> *You fell*
> *And yet you linger in the madness*
> *You glimpsed in passing*
>
> *You live*
> *Your vision burning, its blazes*
> *So long and lasting*
> *To take all the pain away.*

The song had a complicated little guitar riff that was more easily executed on the Stratocaster, my finger calluses not being what they once had been; but by the end, my eyes were closed and the magic was coursing through my fingertips again.

That was probably why I didn't hear the screen door or his footsteps on the porch. When I opened my eyes, I was more than a little startled to see André Ledoux seated next to me, a battered old classical guitar lovingly held in his hands. Panic caused my heart to start—like a runaway horse about to bolt—but he smiled and shook his head. "Just keep doing what you're doing," he said softly. "I'll play around you."

Well, I'll tell you, if heaven is on this earth, that's where I'd found myself late on this sunny June afternoon in the north country. We slipped into a slow twelve-bar blues, and while I held down the bottom, making it nice and solid and safe, his notes soared all over the guitar, reminding me for all the world of the yellow-and-black butterflies dancing around Fred's mock orange earlier in the day.

Then, as if reading my mind, he launched into "Poor Butterfly," drawing out the notes, harmonics dissolving perfectly into the air like a puff of smoke or a beautiful, haunting dream. When my heart was full and happy enough to burst, André glided into an old Elvis tune, "Are You Lonesome Tonight," plucking the strings with all four fingers, a veritable orchestra unto himself, making it the saddest song in the universe.

"Sing it," he whispered, and I did, the way I hadn't sung anything in all the years since my friend and band mate Ron had died, since I'd replaced my dream of playing music with one of survival in a sometimes-hostile world. When I came to the line "Is your heart filled with pain," I felt the truth in it, the world's sorrow sinking into every bone and cell in my body.

We finished up with a rousing version of "Jesus Met the Woman at the Well," which we played faster and faster, André's fingers gliding with consummate ease around the neck of the guitar, playing what seemed like dozens of notes to my one or two. I bravely attempted to keep up, until he'd left me so far behind I soon dissolved into a gale of laughter and screamed, "Enough! I give up!"

Collapsing in utter exhaustion and joy, I lay back on the porch, the guitar across my stomach and a shit-eating grin spread all across my face. André's own smile was as warm as a fresh breeze across the water. I silently thanked whatever spirit guides lived around this lovely man. He had given me music in its purest and most tender form. I would pay him back and pay him well.

# CHAPTER SIX

$\blacksquare$ $\blacksquare$ $\blacksquare$ $\blacksquare$ $\blacksquare$ $\blacksquare$ $\blacksquare$ $\blacksquare$ $\blacksquare$ $\blacksquare$ $\blacksquare$ $\blacksquare$ $\blacksquare$

**A** n d r é was the first to speak of the matters at hand. "I guess you need some answers," he said.

I looked at him and nodded. "And you probably need to get some things off your chest."

He sighed. "I can't seem to get very far without fucking up, try as I might." He pulled at a splinter of wood hanging off the edge of the porch. "I guess you could say that's the story of my life.

"Not all of it," I said. "There's the beautiful part, too."

He met my eyes and his were full of pain and confusion. "You know what *Downbeat* called me? The world's greatest guitar player. Can you believe that?" He shook his head.

I nodded slightly and smiled. "I don't have any trouble with that description. It was a pleasure to have been played clean off the porch by the world's greatest."

"Well, that's a label, like everything else. The reality of my life is that I've been shuffling along for years in small clubs. And *that's* when I've been lucky. Every now and then a festival comes up and someone gets hold of me to perform, but the time in between . . . well, there's mostly me struggling with myself."

I reached around, grabbed a clean rag out of the guitar case, and started rubbing some oil into the fingerboard. It was as good a way to talk as any.

"What I want to know is, why did you decide to come back to Maine, after all these years? What were you looking for here?"

He continued to fiddle with the splinter. "A simpler time, maybe. I felt safe here once."

"And now? How safe do you feel?"

He looked down, worrying his forehead with his thumb and first two fingers. "About as safe as anyone on the lam can feel, I guess. It didn't take me long, did it?" He laughed quietly and bitterly.

I stopped working the oil into the guitar neck and put down the rag. I looked at André for a moment or two and lightly touched his arm, just below where his T-shirt sleeve stopped. "André, what happened? You were doing so well."

"I just had a 'slip'—isn't that what it's called these days? It's quite simple, really."

"Not so simple," I said. "Okay, let's put it another way, then. According to Ernie West, you and the band played a fine gig in Augusta. You were sitting around going over the evening when something happened. You became agitated and appeared to be on a drug you didn't like. You ran out of the place and haven't been back much since. How's that sound?"

"It sounds about right, I guess. I messed up, for one reason or another. It wasn't the place to do it, but what can I say?"

I looked at him in disbelief. Was this the man I had just finished having a spiritual experience with? What was he holding back?

I forged on, hating myself for having to do it this way. "And what about the money taken from Lucie and Carl's house, André? Lucie's in a bit of a jam, I'd say, not to mention a double bind. What was that all about?"

He surrounded himself in a stubborn silence as impenetrable as a vault that had been welded shut. Finally, he appeared to have thought over what he wanted to say. "I feel awful about that, but I needed the money and needed it bad. I knew I could pay her back after the Montreal Jazz Festival."

He was holding back plenty, I was betting, but at least it was an answer.

"I still have most of it, actually. I'll call Lucie and tell her I can pay it back now."

I frowned. "You needed the money, yet you still have it? What gives, André? I'm here to help you, you know, but you've gotta come clean. I feel like I'm floundering here."

He abruptly leaned forward, his elbows on his knees, his head in his hands. I resisted an urge to comfort him, knowing he needed to work through whatever was going on. After a few minutes, he seemed to have made a decision. He sat back up.

"Sometimes things just churn around inside me so much, I can't stand it. I have some idea of what you're trying to do for me, Lil, and I really do appreciate it. It's just that there are things I don't understand fully myself."

"What's it take, then? Foresight? Hindsight? Second sight? 'Cause I could make arrangements, call Ray Charles or something. I just wanna help you. You name it."

At least I'd gotten a smile out of him.

"André, since you have it, why don't you get the money back to Lucie before Carl goes berserk. I could follow you down to Lewiston and even run interference with Carl, if that's what it would take. He doesn't scare me—I've known lots of little guys just like him."

He laughed. "Don't be too sure about that. Carl Pinkham might be one of a kind, not that that would necessarily be a bad thing."

I prodded him with a friendly elbow. "Come on, André. We could call Lucie from here and be back in Lewiston before you know it. Carl will be placated and you can go back to the band that loves you." I crossed my fingers and waited.

"Okay," he said, finally. "Let me call Lucie, and when Tante Eulalie gets back, we could go."

"Just like that?" I could hardly believe it.

"Just like that." He stood up. "Now I believe I need to talk to my little sister."

I stood in the kitchen, nursing a glass of water, while André made things right with his sister. He said he'd see her in the morning, after they'd both had a good night's sleep. "Eulalie sends her love, Luce. She says Uncle Roland wants to hear from you soon. Okay?" He was quiet, listening for a bit, then said, "Me too," and cradled the phone.

André took a deep breath and looked around the kitchen as if he was memorizing its every detail. He saw me watching him and smiled. "Thanks, Lil. I guess it's a good thing you showed up."

"Glad to do it," I said. "Anytime. I'm your biggest fan."

"Well, not the biggest," he said. "There's a guy comes to hear us in Portland who pretty much has that category nailed down."

"Well, I'm your total fan, then. I'm on your side, all the way."

I heard a car pull up and I looked out the kitchen window. "Here comes your aunt. Are we leaving tomorrow? Is that what I heard you say to Lucie? I can get a motel room in town, if that's the case."

He nodded. "We could put you up here, probably. I'm sure Tante Eulalie wouldn't mind."

I stopped him with a wave of the hand. "No, that's okay, André. I'm sure your aunt doesn't want to share you any more than she already has. I'll get a room in the motel by the train station and we could leave from here as early or as late as you'd like."

He nodded. "How about ten A.M.? I'd really like a long, long sleep. I feel like a half-dead dog. Maybe three-quarters."

"That'd be fine. I'm not a morning person, either."

I hesitated. I could hear his aunt's heavy tread on the porch. "André, thanks for agreeing to this. You won't be sorry, I'm sure of it. After today, you get to start all over again. That's not a bad way to go, sometimes."

"I hope that's true," he said. "I really do."

I thanked his aunt for her hospitality and left, feeling that I'd finally been able to make some kind of a difference, in a little corner of the world at least.

From the motel, I called Ernie West to tell him the good news, but it appeared that a message on his machine was the best I could do for now. I told him I'd send him a refund for the remainder of his retainer and that I'd get in touch after I'd seen his friend home. I suspected West was going to be a happy man sooner than he knew.

By mid-evening, I had enjoyed a passable-to-good dinner followed by a night of fairly exciting TV. The Brownville Motel carried the Playboy Channel, something I'd never before experienced. I held my head this way and that until I started to get a crick in my neck. I flipped around the channels but kept coming back to the sex scenes that were there for the watching. One guy, wearing a bland, bored expression, appeared to be rowing a boat—but wait—there was no boat, there was only a woman. Only a woman? What was I saying?

"Are they really doing that?" I asked the empty room. "Is this the real thing or just a cheap simulation?" The room kept its own counsel, no doubt having seen all this and much more.

I kept watching until I grew sleepy during a particularly long "Arabian Nights" sequence. So that's what heteros do, I remember thinking. Poor things, don't you just feel sorry?

I fell asleep and dreamed of playing with the world's greatest guitarist. Now that was more like it.

———————

In the morning, I awoke feeling rested and full of good cheer. After spending about twenty minutes on some stretching exercises in my room, I headed over to the diner for some excellent blueberry pancakes and coffee. The diner crowd seemed to be a mix of small-town folks and men who made their living working in the surrounding woods. I liked what I saw. I made a mental note to come back to the Brownville area sometime and spend a few days exploring.

At ten A.M. sharp, I pulled up into André's aunt's driveway, behind the Buick. When I knocked on the front door, Aunt Eulalie again greeted me, but this time without the suspicion I had first detected on her face. She opened the door wide, inviting me in. "My André, he's a little bit slow, you see, but what can you do, dat's him. When 'e was a boy, it was de same."

"Not to worry," I said. "For him, I don't mind waiting."

Just then André emerged from his room, looking freshly scrubbed and shaved, carrying a canvas bag. "Morning, Lil. I guess I'm about ready to roll, if you are." He smiled. The rest appeared to have done him some good.

"Aren't you forgetting your guitar?" I asked.

He shook his head. "That's an old one I used to play as a kid. Aunt Eulalie keeps it here for me in case I ever hock all my guitars at once. This way, there's always a spare."

The old woman slapped him playfully on the arm. "Stop talking like dat, you incorrigible boy. I keep it only because I don't want to t'row it away. All right, mebbe de next time, I do it, anyway."

"That'll be the day, Tante Eulalie," he said. "Now give me a great big kiss so we can go."

She kissed her nephew on both cheeks, French-style, then bussed him on the forehead, too. I discreetly busied myself examining some old family photographs on the wall while nephew and aunt exchanged a long embrace. Out of the corner of my eye, I could see André rocking his aunt from side to side tenderly. He kissed her again on her cheek and squeezed her tightly one final time.

*"Merci, ma tante.* I don't know what I would do without you," he said huskily.

*"T'es chanceux, mon gars,* because you don't 'ave to find out," she answered, lapsing into French, then remembering me and politely switching back to English as she gave me a big smile. "Now you better go, I t'ink, before this nice girl she get impatient and drive off wit'out you."

I held out my hand to her, but she made a little detour, kissing me on both cheeks as well. I was flattered beyond belief. "You make sure my boy be okay," she said. " 'E's a good boy—just pretending to be a bad boy. His tante Eulalie should know." She tapped her chest, over the heart. "I feel it 'ere."

Her eyes bored into mine, full of feeling and meaning. For a brief moment, I almost thought I could actually see her fierce old will clearly, as if it were a concrete thing that I could reach out and touch.

But what was she trying to make me understand?

Then suddenly, it was over and she was shepherding us out the front door and into our respective cars. I waved to her once more and André honked his horn lightly as he made the corner and we drove out of her sight.

---

The trip back to Lewiston was uneventful enough. It was a hot day, close to ninety degrees, but this time the humidity was low and a steady breeze came out of the north. The skies were a magnificent robin's egg blue, with the occasional stray cloud for contrast. We traveled the two-lane country roads as far as Pittsfield, not in any particular hurry, and from there it made sense to hitch onto I-95, which made the rest of the way a snap. At Waterville, we stopped at a little roadside takeout joint for cold drinks and sat at a picnic table under the trees for a few minutes, enjoying the day.

André had been quiet since we'd stopped. "So what's next for you?" I asked.

He thought a minute. "I need to get myself straight, then I'll see, I guess."

"Have you thought it out?" I asked. "You know what Rocky said: 'Ya gotta plan ahead.' " I attempted a Sylvester Stallone imitation, which was so bad we both laughed.

Something had been bothering me and I wanted to clear the air. "André, about this money deal . . . if you were in trouble before and needed it that badly, how come it's all okay now? Can I help you with something? I've got a little money saved up, if you need it. I'd be honored."

He looked up from his iced tea in surprise. "I take it you don't offer money to *all* your clients. Otherwise, you'd be out of business fast."

"Ah ha," I said, "but there's a wiggle-out clause here— you're not my client, Ernie West is. So I'm free to do what I want. And I want to make sure you're okay so I can come hear you play music 'til the end of my days. There's a selfish motivation here, a very hip nineties kind of thing."

He gave a little smile and shook his head. "I'll be fine, but thanks for asking. It was just something I needed to attend to, but . . ."

"But what?" I prompted him. There was a lot he wasn't telling.

A look crossed over his face so quickly that, had I not been paying such close attention, it would have gone unnoticed. It worried me. "C'mon, André, I have no vested interest in this. Whatever's going on, there are ways to deal with it. You don't have to be alone."

"I'm not so sure about that," he said.

"Well, I am," I said stubbornly.

We passed the next few minutes in silence as thick as a Dutch pea soup. I could take a hint.

"How come you don't play music for a living?" he asked finally. "You could, you know."

"I used to," I said, coolly absorbing the compliment, "but just in a rock band. Didn't work out."

"All music's good; it just depends on what you put into it." He reached across the table and tapped the top of my left hand with his forefinger. "It's in you," he said. "It never goes away. Never. Just remember that."

I had a feeling I was going to.

Then he got up and stretched. "We might as well get going, don't you think?"

I threw my empty cup into a trash barrel next to a nearby stand of young maples. "You want me to go in with you, talk to Lucie or Carl? I'd be glad to. Just say the word."

"Nah," he said. "I'm a big boy. Lucie'll be at home, but Carl won't this time of day. Him, I'll deal with when I'm feeling a little better."

It made sense.

"Lil, you don't have to follow me back. I'll go, I promise. This is out of your way."

Now it was my turn to be stubborn. "Lil Ritchie always gets her man," I said. "She takes him to the door, too."

"What a date," he said. "Okay then. But I need to see Luce alone—we have a lot to talk about."

That was understandable. "I'll just get you there, that's all. Then I'll be on my way."

He nodded, and I got the feeling he didn't really mind my company. "Race you there," he said.

Thirty minutes later, we were driving around the almost-familiar streets of Lewiston. When we came to the turnoff to Lucie's block, André pulled over under a large oak and got out. He stuck his head inside the Subaru.

"I can take it from here," he said.

"You sure?" I asked. "I don't mind waiting in the car until you've talked things over with Lucie."

"Nah, I'm not worried about that. She and I are this tight"—he crossed his middle finger over his index—"and

60

she'll be glad to see her big brother. Really. I've taken enough of your time as it is."

I hesitated, uncertainty written all over my face.

"Lil, I've gotta be a grown man *someday*—might as well start right now." He smiled. "Don't you think?"

There wasn't much I could say. I couldn't live his life for him; I could only do what I could do. Maybe he was right.

"Okay," I said. "But call me if you need me. I'll be there in a flash."

"That, I somehow don't doubt. And thank you, Lil, for all you've done. I really mean it." He squeezed my hand and smiled again, a flash of sweetness mixing in with the sun and the breeze.

I sat there until he'd made the turn leading to his sister's house.

"Take care," I said quietly.

Then I headed back home with André Ledoux's magic in my ears every mile of the way.

———————

The next few days I spent patting myself on the back, a sport little recognized in either the summer or winter Olympics. Most afternoons I would take a lazy drive out to Long Cove and dive into the cold salt water from the rocks, swimming with rapid strokes until I'd warmed up my Southern bones. Then I would spend some time floating on my back, content to watch the ravens, sea gulls, and ospreys go about the business of living while the waves gently, if a little coldly, caressed me.

There was a hill looking out over the cove, a high, fenced-in green pasture with boulders strewn here and there and a couple of magnificent old pine trees stretching to the horizon. The three horses whose summer home the pasture was looked like grace itself, whether running or standing still. I would watch them for what seemed like hours, until the cold began to seep into my muscles and my childhood fantasies of

61

Trigger, Flicka, and Black Beauty threatened to back up, like a kitchen drain full of Brillo pads, and make me blubber like the baby cowboy I still was in some hidden corner of my psyche.

This would be my cue to turn over for one last swim, after which I would drape myself over the hottest rock I could find until I was well-enough baked to drag myself home. It wasn't hard work, but what else was summer for in a state known for its two seasons—winter and the Fourth of July?

I had written Ernie West earlier, sending him back what remained of his money. He'd called me up and thanked me for finding André. He'd sounded good, if a bit rushed. Since then, I'd seen an ad in the paper saying that the André Ledoux Band would be playing in a Portland club a few days later. I'd go down and hear them.

Meanwhile, life went on. A local bookstore hired me to find out how someone was managing to steal entire lots of picture frames and ceramic sculptures from their sales table. I put on a pair of Bermuda shorts and a clashing Hawaiian shirt out of the Goodwill box and spent a few hours at a time pretending to browse and hoping I really looked like a tourist from New Jersey. Since the store was open from nine A.M. to nine P.M., I managed to browse all the way from "Maine Authors," through the history section, the entire collection of sports and how-to books, art history, paperback general fiction, and the classics. By the time I reached the romances, I'd just about lost interest, with some assistance from the subject matter. Strong men named Blake or Eric inevitably rescued damsels named Jennifer or Cassandra either from men named Horst or from their own stupidity. Episodes of thrusting and exploding and burning of one kind or another would inevitably follow. I didn't think I could take much more of this.

Then, midmorning of the fifth day, I recognized a sixty-ish couple from the day before. On a hunch, I edged a little closer to them and watched incredulously as they slipped one item after another into what appeared to be deep pockets sewn into the linings of their clothes—clothes, I might point out, that looked an awful lot like those I was wearing myself. Then they picked up a couple of paperbacks that were on sale and marched right up to the counter like a couple of fat possums carrying their babies on their tails.

I left the store unobtrusively and signaled to the security guard who lurked nearby. Then I sat on a bench just outside the store entrance and waited until they stepped into the hallway, conversing amicably, wreathed in smiles.

I stood up and quickly walked into the man, who flashed me a furious look as the sound of broken porcelain rang throughout the mall. Dave, the security man, took the woman's arm before she was able to veer off toward the mall exit. I smiled meaningfully at them both. "Gotcha," I said. I'd always wanted to say that and now I'd had my chance.

I decided to celebrate my victory with a burger and fries down at Pat's with Molly, the returning mystery woman. We sat at the counter, close to the pie case, all the better to keep a close watch. There were only four pieces left and a woman couldn't be too careful.

Dot brought us Cokes. I took a sip and said casually, "So what's the story? Camping in bug season? Give a girl a break, if I may be so bold."

Molly sighed, and it was a wrong move for someone who was trying to swallow. I patted her on the back until it appeared she would live and breathe again.

"You're not supposed to do that, you know," she said irritably. "You could make someone choke to death. Patting is out—don't you watch 'Rescue 911' anymore?"

"What am I supposed to do—the Heimlich maneuver? Dislodge the piece of soft drink that has cut off your precious wind supply?"

"Oh, fuck off," she said just as Dot arrived with our food.

Dot stepped back and looked at us both. "Ladies, ladies!" she scolded, clucking her tongue. "This is a family operation, don't forget. It's time to put your differences behind you and eat this delicious lunch before it congeals." She laughed.

" 'Before it congeals'?" I asked. "And may I quote you on that?"

Dot gave Molly a level look and said, "Ya know, Molly, sometimes I wonder about your choice in friends. You can't be too careful, ya know, a woman of your standing in the community."

Molly leaned over the counter toward Dot's good ear. "Fuck you, too," she whispered.

Dot's mouth opened in a big round *O* and she shook her head and turned to leave. She was smiling broadly.

"So how was it?" I asked. "You're not very tanned for someone who has been camping on a rock."

"Oh, okay, I give up." Molly sat her burger down in its own little pool of grease and mustard. "What's the use? You can't expect to have a personal life in a town this size. I don't know why I even try."

"You've got your secrets, and I've got mine," I sang. "But not for long, by the looks of you." I waited.

"Okay, but you are sworn to secrecy, or I'll pull out every hair on your head."

"That's no way to treat a lady, but I will agree to your terms, harsh as they are, in the interests of the greater good. Now, what the hell were you doing, really?"

She took a deep breath. "Camping out at Isle au Haut, like I said."

"And?" I prodded.

"With Hugh Pendergrast." She poked me in the ribs with a sharp elbow. "And don't you say a word."

I laughed until I was silenced with another, sharper

poke. "I knew it," she said. "That's why I didn't want to tell you in the first place."

Pendergrast had been Molly's adversary in a lawsuit she had undertaken on behalf of the citizens of Southport, a little town just Down East from us. His clients had wanted to install a coal-fired power-generating plant and the townspeople had opposed it due to the copious amount of smoke it would inflict on this pristine coastal area. Molly had decried the company's methods from the beginning and had had popular support from the newspaper editorialists, as well as from the average person on the street. The case wasn't yet settled.

The reasons for all the secrecy were beginning to dawn on me. "Jesus," I said. "Couldn't you get in trouble for this?"

She moved her plate aside and put her head down on the counter. "I didn't mean for this to happen," she moaned. "I hated him!"

But not enough, apparently. I thought quickly. "You were in the tent the whole time, right? That's why you don't have any tan?"

She moaned a little louder now. "Shhh. Someone will hear."

There was a part of me that still wanted to laugh. Molly was the most levelheaded person I knew; she had a plan for everything. She was rationality personified. She was known professionally for her logical reasoning, her ethical considerations, and her dogged determination. There was nothing that could make her little train jump the tracks—that is, nothing but love, or, apparently, some combination of love and good sex. She couldn't take either for very long.

"So," I whispered, "are you in violation of any lawyer's ethics? Anything that could be used to weaken your case?"

She rolled her eyes and groaned. "I can't think. I'm not sure, but maybe. He's not even my type!"

Her confusion was so atypical and so cute that I stifled an

urge to hug her right there at the counter. It would only serve to make her more miserable.

"Look," I offered. "We live in the boonies, really. All sorts of people know one another and even socialize. Hell, there're cousins and nephews and ex-wives all around the place and nobody thinks twice about it. So how is this different?"

"It just is." She sniffed. "Because it's me, that's why. I don't do this."

"So how was he?" I whispered, again. "Did he melt your socks?"

"Oh God," she moaned.

She didn't have to say more. "C'mon. Let's get you back to the office and you'll feel better. There's a way around everything." And sometimes there really was.

I walked her into the office, whereupon she ran to her answering machine like a thirsty woman to a cold bottle of Corona. She listened and smiled a secret smile when she heard the voice she wanted to hear.

This could be long, I said to myself as I walked from her office into my own. Or it could *seem* long, which is just about as bad. Molly was off and running.

I flopped down into my old leather chair and, putting my feet up on the desk, ran through the messages on my machine. There was nothing there that couldn't wait. I prepared a bill for the bookstore job. Since the store was part of a successful Maine-owned chain, they would be able to pay top dollar, something I would be grateful for the first of the month. I wrote up a report of the job for my own records while all the details were clear. Then I straightened up my desk and updated my files. Unlike Mike Hammer, I had to do all the grunt work myself.

As I glanced through the newspaper, something caught my eye. The André Ledoux Portland gig had been canceled.

The ad I had seen a few days before was still there, but, this time, with a big line running perpendicularly through it, saying, "Canceled." I frowned.

I took out my address book and looked up Ernie West's number. I let the phone ring fifteen times, but apparently not even the answering machine was talking. I dialed Lucie Pinkham and got just about as far. Had Lewiston shut down for the summer?

"Ah jeez," I said. Even Molly was running amok. Here I was, the last stable person in the universe, apparently all alone. It was disconcerting. I looked at my watch and got an idea for a little immediate relief. If I left right now, I could be in my favorite—and the only—gay bar in Bangor in time for happy hour. Sometimes I could be brilliant.

I glanced in at Molly before leaving. She was sitting at her desk, staring down at a pile of papers at least three inches high. Next to that pile were four others that were equally thick. She looked up at me, misery written all over her face. "That the Southport deal?" I nodded toward the desk.

"Yeah. They're trying to paper me to death. They've got corporate backing and I've got little old me. Unfortunately, they've known this from the start. That's how the sharks eat the little fish," she said, smiling sadly.

"Assholes," I said. "You'll just have to be smarter, then."

Molly tapped herself on the head with two fingers. "So far, not so good."

I could tell she needed to get back to work, for many reasons. "I'm going up to the Hollywood," I said. "I'll be back not too late, probably, so call me if you want."

She nodded. "Thanks. Have fun, and watch out for dangerous women." She pronounced it "dang-erous."

"Lord bless us and keep us," I said, "and especially the dang-erous women."

She said her good-byes with a baby wave, her wrist flopping weakly in my direction and a perplexed little smile on her face.

Ah, yes, the Hollywood, I thought as I bounded down the stairs. I could use a little civilized banter with others of my kind.

# CHAPTER SEVEN
■ ■ ■ ■ ■ ■ ■ ■ ■ ■ ■ ■ ■ ■ ■

**A** s
I pulled the Subaru into the lot outside an old redbrick building on the edge of downtown, I looked around for familiar
vehicles. I smiled to myself when I noticed two elderly cars
displaying bumper stickers with pink triangles and a newer
red Chevy Nova with a colorful underwater scene, complete
with coral reefs, fish, and little plastic divers, sitting on the
shelf running along the back window. Terry had been shop-
ping at Newberry's again.

There was no sign in front of the Hollywood, no indication whatsoever to a curious civilian that the door led into a
gay bar. People were cautious and needed to be. In 1985,
Charlie Howard had been badly beaten, then thrown off one
of Bangor's bridges into the Kenduskeag Stream by a few
young men who objected to his sexual inclinations. A lot of
good Maine people of every social stripe had been outraged
and had said so. Others hadn't thought it was such a big deal
and had said so, as well. Now, once a year, a few brave souls
march down the main streets of downtown Bangor on Charlie
Howard Day to celebrate this unlikely martyr's life and to
protest another stupid early death.

As I opened the heavy black-painted door, though, no
outward signs of sadness greeted me. Through the billowing
cigarette smoke, what I saw was about fifteen people, male
and female, sitting in little clusters around the bar and a few

tables. A few of them were laughing and several were accompanying Leslie Gore as she sang, via the jukebox, "It's my party, and I'll cry if I want to."

I slid onto a stool at the bar. "It's a little early for Leslie, isn't it?" I said to the man occupying the next stool.

"It's never too early or too late for Leslie," he said. "We all need to be reminded of her very important and timely message."

"Which is?"

He looked at me. "If you don't know, sister, then I'm certainly not going to tell you." Then he elbowed me playfully. "What brings you here, my good woman? Tired of your own company?"

"More or less," I said. "Whatcha drinking? I'll buy you one."

"Oh, honey," he said, "I've been waiting for a woman like you. I'll take a Beck's, since you're paying. Up 'til now, I've been drinking Bud draft."

"Spend all your money at Newberry's?" I asked. "What did that window display cost you—three ninety-five plus tax?" I signaled to the bartender.

"Nope," he said. "Guess again. Oh, never mind. I'll just tell ya. I barely got out with any change for my five-dollar bill at all. This one was four twenty-five, but I kinda think it was worth it, don't you?"

"Indeed it was," I answered. "Two Becks, please, Irma. How's it going?"

The bartender shrugged and smiled. "Not too bad, I guess. How about yourself, Lil? Keeping busy?"

It was my turn to shrug. "Yeah, with work, I guess. Haven't felt all that social lately."

She nodded. Bartenders didn't have an easy job, either. I knew that Irma and her lover, Lisa, had joined AA a few months back, after a long, hard struggle getting on and falling off the wagon. I hadn't run into Lisa for a while, but Irma was looking healthy and fit.

"Did I tell you that Lisa's graduating next year?" she asked proudly. "Can you believe it? She's the first one in her family even to go to college, much less graduate. Her mom's just about splittin' her seams."

Two years ago, Lisa had entered a program the University of Maine at Orono offered for what they called nontraditional students—people who had, for one reason or another, missed the boat the first time around. Most of these older students were happy to put in the hard work it took to get an education, having lived through a variety of hardships over the years. They were committed in a way few eighteen-year-old freshmen would ever be.

I smiled. "That's really great news, Irma. Tell Lisa we'll throw her one hell of a party when she gets through." I prodded Terry with an elbow. "Won't we, Terry?"

"Huh?" he said. "Sorry. My attention wandered a little for a second or two."

I turned around in the direction he'd been facing. "He's cute, all right, but isn't he a little young for you?"

He frowned and glanced into the mirror facing the bar. "I don't look a day over thirty-five, do I? Especially in this light."

"What light?" I asked. I looked at Irma and winked. "Were you thinking thirty-five dog years or human years? It could make a big difference once you get outside."

"Screw yourself," he said. "Just remember, you ain't no chicken yourself."

He had a point. "Go to it, then. If you don't, somebody else will."

"That's just what I was thinkin'," he said, slipping off the stool.

I turned around and rested my elbows on the worn old

bar, watching the two men dance. Mick Jagger had replaced Leslie, followed by Stevie Wonder. Irma had slipped a dance tape onto the system. When an Aretha Franklin song came on, I decided to join the crowd on the little dance floor. By the time Patti Smith swung into "People have the Power" and "Looking for You (I Was)," we were one solid dancing machine, hot, sweaty, and happy. The old floor swayed to the beat, as it probably had a thousand times. Some night, we'd end up rocking in the basement, most likely.

Winded after a while, I decided to sit out for a couple of numbers. I was joined almost at once by Terry and the good-looking young man, whose name turned out to be Scott. Another friend, Louise, flopped down beside me, wiping her face on her sleeve. "Shit, I used to be able to do this for hours," she said.

"Didn't we all," Terry said. He glanced at Scott. "Not that I still couldn't, if I wanted to."

Louise laughed loudly and I stopped trying to hold back. Scott would just have to get used to us. We passed an hour or so in this way, just a few friends blowing off some steam. The place was filling up. I danced a couple of slow ones with Louise—Joan Armatrading's "Down to Zero" and Rickie Lee Jones's "Don't Let the Sun Catch You Crying." Louise's body was soft and warm, her breasts firmly pressed against my own, and I began to feel an excitement that wasn't coming from the music, as good as that was.

Louise felt it, too. She stepped back a little and looked into my eyes. "How come we never got closer?" she asked. "It's not like either one of us is exactly attached."

I thought about it. "Timing, I suppose. And the fact that I don't like to mess with good friendships. They're hard to come by." I pulled her close again.

But this time, she held back just a little. "Lil, honey, I believe you're givin' me what's called a mixed message, but don't ya think I don't understand. You're waiting for true love, and ain't we all."

"It's probably stupid," I said, the moment spoiled.

"Probably," she agreed. We finished out the dance, then sat down at the table, which had been invaded by three other friends of Terry's whom I knew slightly. One of them, Jack, lived down near Augusta somewhere but visited Bangor fairly often. I'd seen him at the Hollywood a few times and we'd been friendly.

He smiled now and sidled up alongside me. "Woman, if you ain't a sight for sore eyes, I don't know who is," he said. "What's new?"

We spent a few minutes catching up and discreetly watching Terry and Scott getting acquainted. I wished them luck. "So, what's on for the weekend?" he asked now. "Sticking around here, or are you heading for the big city?"

He meant Portland. I shook my head. "I was gonna go down and hear André Ledoux at the Cafe No, but the gig got canceled at the last minute."

"Yeah." He nodded. "Did it ever."

I looked at him in surprise. "How'd you know about it—the papers?" We weren't exactly living in jazz country.

He frowned. "Honey, a boy like me doesn't have to get his news from the papers. He has his sources."

I sat up in my chair. "Like who?" I asked.

He leaned in close. "Like the drummer, Al Sandberg."

I dropped my jaw. "He's gay? I can't believe it!"

He nodded. "I should know. Honey, one thing I know from working in gay bookstores off and on is this: You never can tell. Some of them might be good little Baptists and family men on Sunday morning, but Saturday night, watch out. Not that this applies to Al. It's probably not general knowledge in jazz circles, such as they are, but he's out with his friends and, I might add, with his handsome lovers." He preened for a few seconds, lest I not catch his meaning.

I could hardly wait. "So what happened to the Portland gig?"

"Oh, that's easy. It was set up weeks ago, and nobody remembered to cancel it while André was off wherever he was off to. But now, they're in Montreal practicing for the Jazz Festival. Apparently, André called the guys and off they went. The little slut is probably wooing somebody named Jean-Luc right now."

Of course. I should have thought of it myself. The festival would start in a few days. But why were they there this early? And there was something else.

"What do you mean, 'André called the guys'? Wasn't he around Lewiston? Weren't they already practicing at Ernie's?"

He shook his head. "Something was going on. I don't know what, but it was semi-hush-hush. I wasn't really even supposed to tell anyone where Al was. They kinda sneaked up there to join André, I think."

Now that was the most interesting thing I'd heard all day, maybe all week. But what did it mean?

Jack shook his head again. "Anyone tells you Maine isn't one small town, honey, you tell 'em to talk to me. You can't sneeze but what somebody from fifty miles up the coast offers you a pink hankie."

I felt like I'd just been offered one myself. I thanked Jack for his information, assuring him that Al wouldn't know its source. Suddenly, I found myself in a hurry to leave. I said my good-byes, kissing a few friends and waving to others. And speaking of kisses, Louise's nearly took my breath away, not so much good-bye as hello. I came up for air, flushed and a little confused.

"Whew!" I said unnecessarily.

She looked at me in triumph. "Whatsa matter, Lil, ya feel true love comin' on?"

I didn't have an answer for that one, and she knew it. She laughed softly and squeezed my hand. "Go on, get out of here," she said. "But don't be a stranger now." I left while I still had a mind to.

I drove back to Tillman with my front windows down and the Cowboy Junkies turned up just shy of distortion. Margo's sultry voice swept into the night, her brother Mike's lyrics echoing some sentiments I was having myself:

*This street holds its secrets like a cobra holds its kill.*
*This street minds its business like a jailer minds his jail.*
*That house there is haunted. That door's a portal to hell.*
*This street holds its secrets very well.*

Suddenly, I found myself wondering just how many secrets André Ledoux had failed to reveal to me the other day. And what about the handsome Ernie West—did he have some secrets of his own, as well? And Lucie Pinkham? The list went on and on.

We would see about that. To quote another song, "half truths are always half lies." That, at least, was one thing I *was* sure of on this warm summer night. You had to start somewhere.

---

I checked in on Molly before going home. There were no lights in the office, I could tell from the street, so I swung by her apartment. She greeted me with a gloomy look, and a quick sweep around the living room told me she was still up to her armpits in paper. "There're called interrogatories," she said, "and you don't want to know more—trust me."

I did. Nothing made my eyes glaze over faster than technical law talk. We had a cup of tea together, then I fixed us a couple of tuna sandwiches for supper. I knew that Molly forgot to eat when she was upset, and it was an easy enough way of giving a little support to an old friend.

During the night I slept fitfully, a victim of weird dreams,

75

tuna fish, and rocks in my bed. I tossed and turned, my back starting to act up, no doubt from dancing like a fool after next to no exercise for a few days. Eventually, Littlefield got disgusted and moved downstairs to the couch. I really couldn't blame him. Me, I had no choice but to stay.

In the morning, I looked up Lucie Pinkham's number first thing and started calling her every half-hour. At ten-thirty, she answered, breathless, on the sixth ring. "Pinkham residence," she said, "could you hold for just a second?"

I guessed I'd better, since I heard her set down the receiver with a little thud. She came back quickly, though, with apologies. "Sorry about that, but I was just coming through the door with a couple armloads of groceries. What can I do for you?"

When I told her who I was, though, her voice lost some of its warmth. "Lucie, I'm wondering how André is and I can't seem to get in touch with Ernie West, so I thought I'd just check in with you."

"André is . . . he's fine, I guess. Really, Ms. Ritchie, I'm busy right now."

I pressed on. "I won't take up much time. I'm just doing a little follow-up. How did Carl take the return of your money—is that all straightened out now?"

"The money?" She sounded confused for a moment, then tried to cover. "Oh, yes, that's all fixed. Carl couldn't be happier. Thank you a lot."

Her manner was so different from that of the other day, it almost seemed as if I was talking to another person altogether. Something told me that Lucie Pinkham was hiding plenty. "Lucie," I said, "have you even seen André?"

She hesitated long enough for me to know I'd hit her sore spot. She gamely gave it a try, though. "And . . . when was that? I've seen him, but . . ." She suddenly ran out of gas and stopped. I moved in quickly, before she hung up.

"André didn't come back? Is that what you're trying not to say?"

I heard what sounded like a door slamming somewhere in the house. "I've got to go," she said quietly.

"Okay, but I know he's in Montreal, Lucie. I'll find out what's going on."

"I've got to go!" she said again, and proved it by hanging up on me. I listened to the dial tone for a minute, until it grated on my nerves. Then I called Molly and arranged for the care and feeding of Littlefield for the next few days.

By eleven-thirty I was again on the road, this time headed toward Montreal.

# CHAPTER EIGHT

There are a couple of ways to reach Montreal from Down East Maine, but one of them is such a beautiful drive that I seldom vary my route. I circled around Bangor on 395 again, taking the exit for I-95 South, although at this level the interstate actually shoots straight westward. At Newport, I exited off the big highway, happily in pursuit of the two-lane roads that would take me northwest and into Québec. It would be about a seven-hour drive if I didn't dawdle or run into a moose.

From Newport, I got onto Route 2 and rolled down the windows to enjoy another lovely afternoon. The last few days we'd been lucky, blessedly free of the rain and fog that can dampen our short summers and our spirits. Today the only clouds in the sky were storybook-puffy and harmless, nothing to cause a sun worshiper any needless worry.

Nina Simone's smoky voice kept me company as I sped past rolling land and the occasional old farmhouse, each one a living reminder of what had happened when the early set-tlers abandoned their rocky land to push westward to the plains, where farming brought better results. But the de-scendants of those who stayed still knew a thing or two about growing things, judging by the lush gardens I passed. In six weeks or so, passersby would be invited to help themselves to the sweet, juicy corn that would be piled high on tables near the roadside and they would also be trusted to leave the correct amount of money in exchange.

I drove through the little town of Canaan, whose name conjured up images from my Christian upbringing that I had unsuccessfully tried to bury. Near Skowhegan, the Kennebec River appeared to the left of the highway, wide and powerful, just below a mill where it had been dammed up. I stopped for a couple of minutes to watch it.

Moving water always fires my imagination, and as I sat there with the warm sun on my face, it wasn't hard to visualize the Native Americans who fished these waters not so long ago. I could almost see their birchbark canoes gliding gracefully, almost silently, through the water. It also wasn't hard to imagine the laughter and teasing that would accompany work around the camps as everyone kept busy braiding sweet grass into braids or baskets, smoking fish over fires, or fashioning spear points out of stone. A flatbed truck whizzed by, pulling me out of my reverie, and I thought of a people peacefully and tragically unaware of the troubles about to be rained down upon them like a skyful of tears, from a continent called Europe. I closed the car door and drove on.

I drove through Skowhegan and then Madison, following the Kennebec, which was summer-shallow now, with its rocks and boulders strewn about like handfuls of loose change. Just past Madison, where the paper mill dominates the town, I was reminded again of the lumber barons of the great north woods and the armies of hardworking men who risked their lives daily to get the wood to its destination. Rivers were used much like interstate highways, to float huge pine logs as far as possible downriver, where they were loaded on the ships that would sail them to their buyers. Log drivers would spend their days balancing like trapeze artists, jumping from log to log to keep the flow moving and break up logjams with their pick poles, or, in extreme cases, with sticks of dynamite. Having placed the explosive, the drivers had to scurry and dance to safety on a floor of floating tree trunks, ever mindful of the very real possibility of having a foot or leg pinched off between the logs if they slipped and fell when the dynamite blast broke the jam.

I put on a tape by a Texas group out of Houston called the Banded Geckos, an interesting mix of acoustic swing and pretty folk music. As their clarinet man twisted and turned his notes upside down and into figure eights, I mulled over the questions that were sending me to Montreal in the middle of a hot summer. What the hell was going on with André Ledoux? And why had Ernie West been less than forthcoming with me?

If nothing else, I told myself, I could hear some fine jazz in a great city known for its cultural diversity and ethnic food. Then I could go straight back home. I told myself this, but a voice inside my head was telling me something else. The trouble was, the second voice was woven in and out like a Cuban salsa station on the shortwave radio. I wasn't sure what to make of it.

One thing was clear: André Ledoux had been afraid of something, afraid enough to rob his sister and run to his elderly relative for hiding. I should have wondered why he would so suddenly bend to my wishes and return home so easily. I had been blinded by my own feelings for the man and his music, a mistake I should have known better than to make. I wouldn't make the same mistake twice.

I drove steadily on, stopping only once in Kingfield for a slice of pizza and a Dr. Pepper to go. Soon I reached the point where the Carrabassett River and Route 16 hook up and I began to travel up the Carrabassett Valley, enjoying the scenic surprises at every road twist. At its north end, the road curved onto a gorgeous wetland supporting a huge population of ducks and, I was betting, of mosquitoes as well. A dramatic view of the Bigelow Range claimed my attention, high peaks towering over the gentle, watery landscape below. This was true mountain wilderness.

I passed one-room hunting camps, some with pictures of

black bears out front, some with jumping trout. Huge trucks carrying logs stacked high and often off-kilter were the masters of the highway now, bearing down upon me from behind, fast, forcing me to let them pass. As I neared the crests of hills, I took care to stay on the outside of my lane, in case one of those road hogs hurtling down from Québec came at me from the other direction.

Soon I noticed to my left a body of water the sight of which always made my heart sing. Today the water glistened and sparkled in the strong sunlight, bluer than blue, hugging the highway's curves before dropping out of sight, then appearing again around another hill like an old and loyal friend. I had reached the Chain of Ponds. I pulled over at a familiar spot overlooking the water and feasted my eyes.

It was here that Benedict Arnold and his men had nearly reached the end of their rope in their efforts to get to Québec and enlist the French in the Revolution. Lost, miserable, starving, and frozen, they had learned valuable lessons about fighting the enemy along these ponds, the least of which was the need for either good maps or trustworthy guides. Winter is unforgiving in the north country and a mistake can easily be the last one made. Arnold was lucky, for a time.

I scooted down a bank to change into my bathing suit. I edged into the water cautiously, braving the cold I knew would disappear from my consciousness soon. I dunked my head in and, shivering, began a vigorous swim toward the other side, doing the crawl at first, then the sidestroke, and, after I'd warmed myself up a bit, finishing off with a lazy, slow backstroke. The sun reflected off the water, making it look like a sea of crystals, blinding me with its glare. But I didn't care.

When I'd had enough, I swam for shore and let the sun do its job drying me off. I zipped up my jeans, threw my T-shirt back on, and combed the hair out of my face with my fingers. A few minutes later I was crossing the border into

Québec, waved on my way after just a few questions by a customs man with a trim little mustache and a pronounced Gallic inflection to his good English. I was going up to the metropolis of French Canada on a visit, to listen to world-class jazz, to see a friend or two, to eat souvlaki, and to drink some authentic café au lait, I told him. Then I was coming right back home.

This is what I told him, and this is what I told myself.

---

As soon as I crossed the border, the entire landscape abruptly changed, as if the land itself knew that it was a part of something other than the United States of America. The road wound around for a bit, then began to climb up and up, until the old Subaru started to complain. I was still in the Appalachian foothills, but in Canada—same mountain system, different country. I began to understand a little how Europeans might feel about geography.

At the crest of the highest hill, the view I saw surprised and delighted me as it never failed to do. The road stretched out below as straight as a preacher's heart, in a line so unerring that I could have driven it with my eyes shut. Fertile farmland lay before me, the farms stretching in narrow strips on either side of the roadway. I knew there was a reason why the road didn't follow the lay of the land, as it would have only a few miles across the border: It had originally been granted by the King of France to seigneurs who divided it between those who opened it up and farmed it. In turn, these farmers divided the land up further between their sons, always in long strips so that the farmhouses could be near the road and not as isolated as if they had been in the middle of vast acres. Depending upon which crop the farmers were growing, the colors of the strips would vary nicely, and from a distance, the landscape often looked to me like a painting by Cézanne.

I was entering the region called the Eastern Townships.

It is now populated by a mix of French and English speakers, the English having come in the back door, from the south, not wishing to foresake the British Crown at the time of the American Revolution. Those who fled across the border to Canada were welcomed by the king's representatives there. The British Empire Loyalists thrived in their new country and their descendants, long since fully Canadian, felt Québec was home just as strongly as did their French-speaking neighbors. So worked the passage of time.

The route from the border town of Woburn shot straight westward and now the Subaru and I flew down long grades that dipped low into the small villages huddled in the valleys, gathering whatever speed we could work up for the long climb back up the next hill.

If the lay of the land was noticeably different to a girl from the country to its south, so were the houses. Old-style Québec farmhouses are unique, with their tin roofs pitched down at a sharp angle, then dipping back up in a graceful curve at the last moment. Newer houses made valiant attempts to duplicate this traditional style, often unsuccessfully, the pitch or the curve ending up several crucial degrees off. This mitigated success on the architectural side was compensated for by the owners' attempts to beautify whatever space they owned or lived in. Slovenly kept property stood out like a redheaded stepchild in the Québec countryside.

Large granite Catholic churches with shiny tin roofs and graceful steeples dominated in even the smallest villages. Unlike among Puritans, whose notions I felt still ruled much of the lower forty-eight, many villages here could offer a weary traveler a drink in a bar with a topless or even naked dancer, often within spitting distance of the church.

I passed Christmas-tree farms and fish hatcheries, neighboring on lush dairy farms. Herds of holsteins stood around like groups of teenagers hanging out on Saturday night.

Some were munching, a few were lying down, and always one or two old girls lazed about in a shallow pond, up to their bellies in the cool water. It didn't look like a hard life.

At Lennoxville, I gassed up and almost passed out when I saw how much gasoline was going to cost me in Québec. I grabbed a *hambourgeois* "all dressed" and *patate frite* at a Casse-Croute, noticing that most of the people I saw seemed to be bilingual, without any particular fuss being made about it. Although the language issue has been hotly debated throughout Québec's history, and still is, a friend had once told me that the farmers who populate this area had quietly solved their problems by way of needing each other for survival. One man owned the hay baler and his neighbor needed to borrow it, so he paid him back by helping him with his own harvest. For these practical exchanges, they had used whatever bits of each other's language they knew. It was a good distance to any big city and, in this rural area at least, people had found ways to keep the peace. Succeeding generations had grown up together and today many young parents showed pride in their children's bilingualism.

The route from Lennoxville to Ayer's Cliff crossed one of the most beautiful rural areas I had seen. I drove through it slowly, admiring the richness of the soil, imagining the simple pleasures life here would bring. At a sign advertising a pick-your-own strawberry farm, I stifled an impulse to veer off and eat my way through a pint of the fresh fruit. Soon after that, I spotted a large lake off a ways to my right and recognized Lake Massawippi, which I had been told was an Indian word for "deep waters." Gentle hills on the horizon—ripplings still of the Appalachians—tapered behind the long lake, framing it in my mind like a fondly remembered photograph.

Taking a right turn towards Ayer's Cliff, I drove briefly under a canopy of large elms standing sentry in front of two Loyalist churches, their grounds, and an old cemetery. I caught a glimpse of a little flock of goldfinches riding the tops of tall wild grasses at the edge of a yard. This was rich bird country, with red-winged blackbirds flashing their colors, as well as eastern kingbirds and cedar waxwings.

In Ayer's Cliff, I got out of the car and stretched some of the stiffness from my legs and back, then went into a store to get a bottle of Vichy water for the road. It seemed a pleasant little village. If I ever move out of Maine, I plan to check it out.

From Ayer's Cliff, I took a connecting highway through more green farmland. Near a turnoff for Magog, I noticed gulls following a tractor, greedily taking advantage of the worms a farmer had inadvertently dug up for their dinner. Then, before I knew it, I was on the autoroute and traffic was whizzing around me. The highway signs were all in French, which wasn't really a problem, but the speed-limit signs made me wish I'd paid attention in at least one math class. Let's see, I thought, a hundred kilometers an hour must be something like—what? I sped up to sixty-five, which seemed a safe guess, but still the Subaru and I were lollygagging about compared to the rest of the traffic, possibly on its way to a Grand Prix competition.

The highway climbed again, past a lovely small mountain called Mount Orford and then another, Bromont, with its ski-slope-scarred face and its Olympic equestrian facilities. The Appalachian foothills now had almost exhausted their northward push and Vermont's Green Mountains, which I could see on my left horizon, were higher than these Québec sisters. When the highway straightened out, it did so with a vengeance, and I found myself on a vast plain with large agricultural operations on either side of the road. An old tractor-trailer body sat in the middle of one of the fields, with large letters advertising MEUBLES. Furniture? I thought. Well, I suppose it could pay to diversify.

Now isolated odd mounds loomed in the distance, seeming to rise out of the plain, separated from their cousins by geology and fate. With names like Mont Saint-Hilaire, Mont Saint-Grégoire, and Rougemont, they were the main attraction of the Montérégie, a region beloved of Montrealers because it was both close and familiar; you could hike and fish there in the summer, pick apples in the fall, ski in the winter, and go maple sugaring in the early spring.

I was close to the city now and traffic was thickening considerably. I watched nervously as drivers wove in and out of it, tailgating and switching lanes with great suddenness at a rate of speed that caused my heart to lurch from time to time. I've done my share of city driving, but it had been a while. I crossed over to Montreal on the Champlain Bridge, riding high above the mighty St. Lawrence River, above the locks of the St. Lawrence Seaway, which connects the Great Lakes to the Atlantic, above large ships, marinas, and sailboats, feeling excitement stir as I looked out on the impressive skyline before me. Newer skyscrapers like the black-glassed Tour de la Bourse, Place Ville-Marie, the Bell Canada building, and the Château Champlain with its half-moon windows now dwarfed the fine seventeenth-century buildings miraculously still tucked around their bases.

I followed the Centreville signs and quickly found myself in the heart of downtown Montreal. People were getting off work and men with loosened ties were heading into the bars and outdoor cafés that lined the narrow streets. The women were dressed to the nines, wearing fashionable suits, very high heels, and skillfully applied makeup. This could be interesting, I thought—women with makeup. Indeed.

With a start, I realized I'd almost rammed into a stopped taxi. Flustered and cursing softly under my breath, I watched as a young dark-haired beauty disengaged herself from the beaten-up old cab, miles of long legs followed by the rest of her. I sat there stupidly until impatient honking behind me said it was time to move on. Lillian, you're gonna have to hold down your girl-watching, I thought, or you ain't gonna get a damned thing done.

I crossed downtown proper that way, in stops and starts, noticing all the different kinds of people who never made their way down to Maine—Asians and Africans, women in flowered saris, men in turbans. Through my rolled-down car windows, I heard snatches of conversation in languages I couldn't begin to identify.

I drove up Sherbrooke and turned onto St-Denis, looking for a parking space near a café with outside seating. Near the corner of Roy and St-Denis, I lucked out and found an empty table near a group of trendy-looking youths. I smiled at the waiter, feeling cosmopolitan as all hell.

"And what can I get you?" he said.

"*Je voudrais un café au lait et un croissant, s'il vous plaît,*" I said suavely in my near-perfect French. The waiter looked at me with pity in his eyes. "And would you like anything else, madame? Is that all?"

Did I have a great big *E* for English tattooed on my forehead? How was I going to practice my French if everybody insisted in talking to me in English?

"*Non, merci,*" I said bravely, fanning myself in an exaggerated manner. "*Mais oui, c'est chaud aujourd'hui.*" I noticed that the nearest youth was smiling.

The waiter raised an eyebrow at me before walking off, pad in hand. He could have an intelligent conversation anywhere, I thought, perhaps just a shade defensively.

"H'it wasn't too bad," my neighbor said. "If you practice a little bit, you'll get better!"

I smiled back at him gratefully. I was in the great city of Montreal and life was good.

# CHAPTER NINE

W h e n
my coffee was gone and the croissant was just a memory, I got back into the Subaru and, making an illegal left off St-Denis, headed west on Roy. There, I exercised my rights as an alien to double-park in front of a little *dépanneur* while I ducked in for a pack of Gitanes and a six-pack of Brador. While keeping a nervous eye on the car, I made a quick call from the pay phone outside the store.

I drove down the narrow little streets in second gear, taking in a Montreal summer's evening in what was known locally as Balconville. It was an old joke that still worked, as whole families traded the oppressive heat inside their apartments for the little bits of breeze that could be found on their balconies and front stoops. It went like this: Where did you go on your vacation? The answer: Balconville.

The names of the streets I passed were familiar now, like an old song I hadn't heard in a while—Henri-Julien, Laval, and Hôtel-de-Ville. I took a right onto rue de Bullion, where dozens of eyes followed the old car's movements. Dark, swarthy men leaned against the old brick buildings here, smoking and talking in little groups. The women who walked by were mostly dressed in black, from the scarves that covered their hair to the shoes on their feet, in a lifetime of mourning for one distant relative or another. This is an old immigrant neighborhood. In a few years the Portuguese and Haitians living here will be gone, leaving these streets to other newly arrived ethnic groups.

I squeezed into a parking space between Napoléon and Duluth and sat in the car for a few minutes, listening to the radio while changing my inner gears. The tall old building before me, where my friend Raymond still lived, was the same, the one lone holdout from cosmetic surgery on the block. I wondered briefly what was holding it up. Its steep, winding outside staircase was missing some wrought iron on its railings, I noticed, and only a few of the rickety-looking steps were covered with carpet. The front of the building was still littered with loose garbage, as if some invisible wind had sucked it there with a magnet and let it go. A scrawny, beat-up yellow cat glanced once over its shoulder before slipping soundlessly through a hole in the fence leading into a back courtyard. I gave silent thanks that Littlefield didn't have to face that particular tough guy in battle.

But moments later, this was all forgotten as a second-floor door was flung open and I was gripped in a breath-defying hug. Quickly relieved of my bags, I followed my friend into a spotless apartment where polished wood floors were the name of the game. Antique French-Canadian country furniture made of white pine filled the rooms, as did old quilts on the walls, quilts that I knew had been made with love by my host's mother when she was a young girl in the mountains.

Now, flopping into an overstuffed chair in the living room, beer and cigarette in hand, I gazed fondly at my old friend. Sprawled shoeless on the couch, he eyed me as well, nodding slightly. "Jesus, Raymond, you don't look a bit different, I swear."

He smiled. "If you ignore the fact that my forehead and hairline have merged into the top of my head."

I laughed. "I wasn't gonna mention that. Besides, you look as handsome as ever."

"You look good, too, Lil, healthy and happy and relaxed. It's good to see, especially these days."

He didn't have to tell me what he meant by "these days," during this plague of AIDS. "And you?" I said. "You're doing okay?"

"So far, so good," he said. "I enjoy myself when I can. I work hard and play hard and see my friends a lot." He shrugged. "You just do the best you can do."

I nodded. "I've lost a couple of friends that I know of and I'm getting scared to check on the ones I haven't seen in a while."

"It's a bitch. I used to try to figure out why this was happening to us, and I think that's how I lost my hair. Then one day I realized, Honey, there just ain't no rhyme nor reason, and that took care of some of the mental masturbation that goes along with the rest of it. Now I just try to help out. We survive in whatever ways we can. It took me a long time to get to that place, mind you." He sighed.

I raised my beer to him in a toast. "To old friends, wherever they may be." We drank.

We gossiped a while, drinking and smoking a little. I was sure that Raymond wasn't any more of a current smoker than I was, but it had been something we'd done together when we were younger. It was fun every once in a while to step outside the boundaries we set for ourselves in everyday life.

"Still playing music?" I asked now. We had been involved in a coffeehouse together when we were both still in our teens. Raymond had come up to Charlottesville from Georgia to attend the university and had quickly found a music crowd with which to neglect his studies. We had spent the next couple of years jamming far into the night, until the draft board caught up with him. Finally, running out of options, he had fled to Canada and hadn't seen fit to turn his back on it yet.

He shook his head. "Not much," he said. "The restaurant keeps me pretty busy and I got out of the habit, I guess. I never was as serious about it as you, anyway."

I laughed. "I remember. We used to fight about that. I said if you didn't do it with all your heart, you shouldn't do it. You said it was nobody's business how much anyone put into their music—that it was still theirs."

"What did we know?" he said now. "How about you? Playing?"

"Sore subject," I said, "but as usual I'm all ears. I'll listen to anything, at least once."

"I won't." He laughed. "I'm too old and cranky even to try to understand rap music, and I still hate heavy metal. Leave it to the kids; they can take it."

When we were gossiped out, he asked me, "So what are you up here for? Can I help you out?"

I cleared my throat. "There may be something I need to investigate. Maybe not. But I'd like to find out." I told him what had happened so far.

"You're in luck, Ritchie. I know half the jazz musicians in town because of Le Bayou Fumeux. I offer special discount dinners to anyone appearing at the Jazz Festival—I've done it for several years—so by now I have a loyal following. You want to know where André Ledoux is staying, I can find it out in two phone calls."

"You always did know everybody," I said. "Too bad you didn't go into politics."

"Shit. That'll be the day. Hold on, Lil, I'll be right back."

Five minutes later he returned to the room, smiling widely, bouncing on the balls of his feet like a young athlete, which was a future he had narrowly escaped. He waved a piece of paper in my face, then teasing, he pulled it back. "A joint first," he said. "Then the address, phone number, and another beer and cigarette."

"You're a regular prince," I said, taking off my sneakers and stretching out on the couch. Tomorrow would be soon enough.

He did a pirouette once around the room, eyes rolled comically up in his head, his eyelashes fluttering rapidly. "Don't you mean princess, my good woman?"

"Hell no," I said, throwing a pillow at him. "Raymond, Raymond," I said happily, "however *did* we escape the way we did?"

"We were young and gay, my dear, and they were glad to see us go. Now stay right there and I'm gonna knock your socks off." He reached under the chair for his stash. I eyed the piece of paper that sat on the coffee table, wondering where it would lead me.

Tomorrow.

---

The address where André and the band were rehearsing was close by, on St-Laurent, between Pine and Prince Arthur. It was well within walking distance. After two cups of Raymond's espresso and a breakfast of Portuguese corn bread and cheese, I was ready for a stroll.

Raymond had long since stumbled out, hung over, to start the night's specials his restaurant would feature. A good three years before the Cajun fad hit hard in the States, he'd had the idea of opening a Cajun restaurant in Montreal and had found an enthusiastic clientele from the start. Now he was enjoying enough success to employ a couple of cooks to handle the nightly rush, which allowed him to come in earlier and cook the specials the place was known for: shrimp-and-sausage gumbo, crab étouffée, and jambalaya. Montrealers couldn't get enough of that exotic food and the irony that went with it. If some of their Acadian ancestors hadn't gotten wind of the cruel exile that the Brits were getting ready to perpetrate in 1755 and fled to Québec, they could have found themselves eating this food in Lafayette or Breaux Bridge,

Louisiana, right now, calling it their mama's home cooking. It was hot already and I was betting it would be a stinker by midafternoon, so I dressed for comfort, in baggy shorts and a faded, loose Hawaiian shirt. I walked slowly down de Bullion and turned west on Napoléon, headed for The Main. As I crossed over the small streets that run parallel to de Bullion, Coloniale, and St-Dominique, I thought about what this section of the city meant to its citizenry.

St-Laurent was a long street that covered most of the city, running northwesterly from close to the St. Lawrence River all the way up to the Rivière-des-Prairies at the island's outer edge. But it's more than a street. The Main represents the division between East and West, the rich and the poor, and it's known waves of immigrants who have called it home for several generations. Walking down it now, I marveled at the kosher shops whose proprietors displayed plucked chickens hanging upside down by their feet. I passed the St. Lawrence Bakery, where Eastern Europeans with tattooed numbers on their wrists waited in line for the best rye bread to be found in the city. Spice shops offering the finest saffron and other Eastern and Mediterranean flavors sat alongside small stores run by Greeks or Armenians, specializing in fresh vegetables and fruit from Israel, with five or six kinds of olives, dill pickles, and feta cheese in big wooden barrels.

In between the food stores were odd little shops crammed with every gadget you could think of, from pieces of pipe and wire and rubber to clothes with a distinctly other-worldly bent. Mannequins in the windows, heavily made up with colors ranging from pinks and reds to out-and-out purples, mimed the face makeup of many of the young women I passed on the street. Indian restaurants sat alongside delicatessens selling smoked meat, near magazine stands selling entertainment and news from home in ten or twelve languages. I passed a gay bookstore with a lively window display and made a note to return there sometime to browse.

93

It was quite a trick walking down The Main, fully feeling its flavor while keeping in mind the business at hand. I conjured up a few possible scenarios I might face in a couple of minutes but finally decided I would play it by ear. André trusted me, at least a little, and I'd had a good contact with Ernie West. Of course, that hadn't stopped either one of them from lying to my face—and behind my back as well, for all I knew. But I was a professional and I would attempt to complete my job in a way that would satisfy me.

Despite the noise of the street, I could hear the music wafting down from the open third-story windows of the building. What I noticed was mostly drums, although I could occasionally hear a snatch of a guitar phrase before the wind or a loud delivery van would take the sound away. I grabbed a couple of cold bottles of Perrier and bounded up the stairs.

No one responded to my knock, which probably hadn't been heard, so I turned the knob and walked in. What I saw was a high-ceilinged loft outfitted with modern chrome and leather furniture, with musical equipment taking up most of the space around the central part of the room. To one side were a small kitchen and dining area and a door that probably led to a bathroom. One bedroom was apparently to the front of the building, cater-cornered and up a step—I could see the foot end of a bed sticking out. I didn't have time to make more observations, because suddenly the music petered out and all eyes were on me.

Al Sandberg, the drummer, nodded at me in a friendly manner, then went about working on a complicated drum-roll, moving his sticks skillfully from the snare drum across two toms and ending up on a large cymbal with a surprisingly delicate sound. Ernie West gave me a shamefaced look before he could muster a smile, and André Ledoux shunned all eye contact for the moment, looking the picture of misery.

For my part, I stood there stupidly, like a parent at a teenaged necking party, not sure whether to come or to go.

It somehow seemed too late to do either with any sense of decorum. But no, that was just the Southern-woman-up-bringing thing coming to the fore. I would have to do better, to call up who I was at this moment in time. It wasn't ever easy. I swallowed my culture like a snake eating a rat and smiled at the three men.

"Hello, boys," I said. "I think we need to talk, don't you?"

After a meaningful look among them, followed by an audible sigh from André, Ernie West leaned his bass carefully against the wall. André reached over to unplug his amp, then sat there scratching his head. The drummer, blissfully un-aware, kept working his sticks against the skins, rat-a-tat-tat and then some.

---

"Let me get this straight," I said, looking Ernie West in the eye. "André called you from here, telling you to come up, to keep it quiet, and you automatically did what he said without a whimper."

We were seated in a café across the street, surrounded by ferns and light-colored wood, having three-dollar cups of coffee served to us by a snotty waiter.

André cleared his throat and I looked at him instead. "Don't give Ernie too much shit," he said, giving me an odd little smile. "He tried to talk me out of it, but he couldn't. I did what I thought was best and so did he. I'm sorry we both lied to you, though. I hated to do it, if it makes you feel any better."

"I'll feel better when I know what the hell's going on," I said. "If you let me in on whatever it is, you wouldn't have to hide out here like little kids."

André looked over at Ernie, who shrugged slightly and gave a hand gesture that meant, It's up to you. We sat there like that for a little bit until my annoyance got the better of me. I got up from my chair abruptly.

"Just forget it. I'll get some tickets to the festival, since I'm here, anyway. It's not like I didn't have anything better to do." I started to walk off, truly angry, leaving them with the check. It served them right.

Ernie caught up with me before I'd made it out the door. He grabbed me lightly by the sleeve. "Lil, I'm sorry. I don't even know the whole story, but I know André's scared. That's why I came and that's why I lied to you."

I hesitated, my anger not quite spent. I nodded in André's direction. "What about him? Does he want some help, or was I just playing some kind of game with him down in Brownville?"

Now, I suddenly realized where my anger was coming from. I'd had a truly wonderful moment with André on his aunt's porch, a musical gift that I'd remember all my life. But since I'd found out he'd outfoxed me, I'd felt used, wondering whether I'd only made up the moment out of need.

I glanced over at André, who'd stood up from the table and was watching my exchange with Ernie. He nodded to me once, humbly. Suddenly, I saw a shy, slightly built, balding man, someone whose life had never given him the strength to deal with his miraculous talent. Music was all he'd had, and now something or someone was scaring him enough to make him run toward the only thing that had ever given him any real, lasting comfort in this world. Who was I to say that he didn't have that right?

I turned around and walked back to the table. André now lit a cigarette and blew the smoke toward the ceiling in a thin stream. "I'm sorry I didn't come straight with you, Lil. The real truth is that someone slipped me something at the club in Augusta. LSD, I think. I kinda freaked."

So *that* was what had happened. He'd been straight for months and someone had taken care of that.

"Do you suspect anyone in particular, André?" I asked softly.

96

He shook his head too quickly. "No one. I don't know who would hate me enough to do that to me. It's not as if I didn't take psychedelics when I was younger—we all did, I guess—but I never took them without being prepared. Whatever it was, it threw me for a loop."

"And it started you drinking," I reminded him.

He nodded slowly. "I hardly knew who I was for a couple of days. I'd struggled to be straight and hadn't even had a joint or anything for months. Suddenly, I was hallucinating some bad shit and I thought I'd gone crazy. I guess I was right, for a few days there." He looked down at the table.

"Okay," I said, "that makes sense. But why did you steal the money from Lucie and Carl? Do you remember?"

He looked so ashamed that I was almost sorry I'd brought it up. "I just panicked. I thought that if someone was going to that much trouble to fuck me up, I'd better get out of their way fast. I've known some bad dudes in my time."

I thought about that for a few moments. "But not anymore, am I right? You don't have dealers waiting backstage for you these days, do you?"

He shook his head again.

I looked over at Ernie, who didn't look at all surprised. So he'd known what André was telling me. "How long have you known about this, Ernie?" I asked now.

"Just since I got up here. When I hired you, I told you what I knew at the time. When André asked me to come up to Montreal and to keep it mum, he said he'd explain things when I got here, and that's the first I knew of it."

"Do you have any ideas about who would stand to gain from this? Did you notice anybody suspicious hanging around the club?"

"Nope, but I sure wish I had," he said darkly.

"Who did you talk to after the gig? Or do you think the drug was slipped to you earlier?"

André thought about that for a minute. "It could've

happened during the break. I started feeling a buzz as soon as we sat down after the last set. Sometimes it can take a while to kick in."

"Had you eaten before you played?"

"Yeah. It was part of our arrangement with the club owner. He fed us after we'd done the sound check, around seven or so. We all had lasagna and a salad, I think."

I tried to think back to the wild psychedelic days of my youth. André was right—LSD definitely kicked in faster when you hadn't eaten first. "What did you do on your break?" I asked the two men.

They looked at each other. "The usual," Ernie answered. "We chatted with the manager some, at a table set aside for the band. Al and I probably had a beer and André usually stuck with club soda or a Pepsi." André nodded his agreement.

"Did anyone else come over to the table?"

"Just a couple of fans who showed up pretty often. One of the guys does a jazz show at WERU and it's fun to connect with him because he's so knowledgeable about the music."

I took out my notebook. "Let me get his name, then, in case he noticed anything you didn't. I'll check with him when I go back. Meanwhile, I have a suggestion, André. Let me hang around here in the background and make sure nothing like this happens during the festival. We can make up some excuse about why I'm lurking around and I'll be able to keep my eyes on things. Whatcha say?"

Both men were beginning to look a little relieved, I noticed. "Okay," André said, "but I'm not really worried here. Montreal's always been good luck for me."

"And I'm sure it will be this time, too." I smiled. "Just think of me as your insurance policy or something."

Ernie spoke now. "I can pay you more money, Lil. You've earned it already."

"Let me see how it goes," I said. "I want to hear the

music anyway and this is a good excuse to hang around with some musicians."

Both men laughed. "Some people would rather be fried in oil than do that very thing," Ernie said.

"Not me. How about we say I'm a journalist writing about André's music? That'll give me a legitimate reason to stick close."

André looked pleased. I'd forgotten that there had been long, empty spaces between praise for the man's music throughout his career. "Okay, I guess."

I walked over to the loft with them. Before going up the stairs, I took André aside one last time. We leaned against opposite walls in the narrow hallway, facing, while I asked him my question. "You're sure you don't know who did this to you, André?"

Maybe it was because I was looking for it, but I thought I saw the evasive look that he'd shown me one time before, at his aunt's house in Brownville. He shook his head no, though.

I was beginning to feel like a mother grilling her teenage kid. "You'd tell me if you knew, wouldn't you?"

"If I knew for certain, I would," he admitted.

"For certain," I repeated sluggishly. "So you *do* suspect someone in particular. Does Ernie know that?"

"I don't even know it myself," he said, and vanished up the stairs.

I sat down on a bottom step, taking a five-minute breather. I had a feeling I was going to earn it.

# CHAPTER TEN

R aymond
and I saw each other so little during the next few days that we
took to leaving each other notes. After my talk with André and
Ernie, I'd gone back to the apartment on de Bullion for some
of my life-support system—a book, Canadian writer Keith
Maillard's *Two Strand River*, in case I got tired of watching
rehearsals; a change of clothes a tiny bit more dressy than
shorts and a Hawaiian shirt; and a tin of Virginia boiled
peanuts my mother had recently sent me. You never know
when hunger can strike. I also picked up a large notebook,
hoping it would make me look more like a journalist than a
snoop. I scribbled a note to Raymond and headed back to the
loft on St-Laurent. I was ready for business.

For two days, I sat, stretched out on the couch, paced,
and perched on a windowsill as the band put in the long,
grueling hours of practice it would take to get ready for one
of the best jazz festivals in the world. André was tireless as he
played whole songs, snatches of songs, phrases, and bars over
and over again, sometimes alone but often with just the bass
as they worked out the stops and changes to the newer material. Al Sandberg was a drum wizard, which made him fun to
watch and even more delightful to hear. Sometimes it seemed
he would repeat a pattern only for a few bars before he would
switch fluidly from the snare drum to a percussion instru-

ment, to a whistle, to a rattle, to a rain stick while pulling out yet another rhythm from the ozone, something Brazilian or Cuban or Cajunto. When things were really cooking, Al would stare into space with a silly half grin on his face, humming along in an atonal growl, which, oddly, only seemed to add to the music.

Ernie West was calm and patient and equally skilled at plucking or bowing his bass. He was tall enough to sit on a high stool while he played, and often, as he cradled his instrument, his looks would put me in mind of a graceful blue heron. Although their music had always swept me away, I began to notice the subtle changes that come from hard work and good chemistry. André's playing took on a wild quality that I'd never before heard him express, using the electric capabilities of his Gibson ES-335 to turn his usually mellow sound inside out and raw, then pulling back at the last moment to rein himself in with a beautiful chord progression or single-note melody.

The traffic inside the loft had been minimal. A few people dropped by, mostly having business pertaining to the festival, as well as a couple of members of the local press. I met a handful of musician friends of André's. I was introduced as a journalist from a magazine called *New England Jazz* and was hoping no one would try to buy a subscription anytime soon. Maybe that could be my next career.

When the guys were safely tucked into bed at three or four A.M., I'd sprint back to Raymond's couch, where I'd hole up until breakfast time. We dined on bagels from one of the last brick-oven bakeries in Canada, standing in line while one mustachioed man wrestled giant armloads of dough into bagel shapes and dipped them briefly into boiling water, after which the second worker coated the steaming pieces of dough with sesame or poppy seeds and slipped them on a plank into the blazing fire. For a few minutes, all talking would stop among the hungry standing in line and mouths would water as the bagels were retrieved and put into brown bags, a dozen at a time, still hot.

Lunch or dinner, we'd often sneak over to a Greek joint on St-Viateur, across from the bagel shop, that served the best souvlakis and donors in town. The place had once been recommended to me by a young Greek woman I met at a St. Patrick's Day party. She had mentioned their authentic yogurt sauce, which, according to her, was the only one in town that was "right." Chunks of lamb, tomatoes, and onions were rolled up in a piece of pita bread and slathered with the oregano-flavored sauce, accompanied if you wished by large Greek salads with all the greenery left out and just the olives, tomatoes, onions, and feta pulling their own weight.

The days with the musicians were long but pleasant enough. Although it was true that I was working, I never quite lost sight of the fact that I was enjoying a unique time with one of my musical heroes. André was mellowing and visibly relaxing as he threw himself more and more into the music. I attributed some of this to the fact that he was finally getting a bit of the recognition he deserved and not having to worry about a sinister LSD giver or, for a time, a furious brother-in-law. I was glad to share in any part of this, his moment of grace, no matter how short it might be.

On the morning of the third day, I answered a knock at the door during a tender version of "Secret Love." I saw before me a tall woman with wavy long brown hair and a strong nose and chin. She was carrying a guitar case, dressed in jeans and a Mexican cotton shirt, and looked vaguely familiar. For a moment, she peered around me, taking in the song and its players, before resting her gaze on me. She smiled and, setting down her guitar, extended her hand. "I'm Lee Wilder," she said. "André's expecting me sometime today, so I thought I might as well go ahead and stop by early."

Lee Wilder! Even her handshake gave me a little electrical jolt. I'd been hearing wonderful things about her playing for the last couple of years but so far had only been lucky enough to hear a tune or two on WERU. She'd done little recording so far, but word of mouth had done its job. She was young and some of the old boys of jazz had been praising her in print, something about as unusual as northern lights at noon. I stepped aside and let her into the room.

André and the guys hadn't noticed her arrival, so they continued their playing. I thought about interrupting, but, with a smile, she shook her head no. She took a seat I'd offered on the couch and sat back to enjoy the music, like any fan. "You with the band?" she asked in a near-whisper. I gave her my name and lied about my credentials. *"New England Jazz?* Hmmm. Sorry, but I can't place it." Well, it was no wonder, I thought, since it didn't exist as far as I knew. "I'd love to see an issue, though," she said enthusiastically.

Just then, André looked up and noticed Lee's presence. "Lee! All right! Now we're gonna cook." He put down his guitar and, with a flourish, bowed deeply from the waist. It was such an uncharacteristic gesture from this introverted man that I had to laugh. With a couple of long steps Lee met him halfway, bowing back. Ernie and Al looked on for a moment, grinning, before setting their instruments aside to greet their visitor.

André looked toward me now and his smile was like a string of sunny days after a month of fog and rain. "Lil, did I tell you? Lee's gonna sit in with us on Sunday night. This is a real treat. Two guitars, bass, and drums—it's crazy, man, but you just wait!"

It was out there, all right, I thought, but with two masters, it would be plenty interesting at the very least. The more usual thing would have been with two solo guitars, the way Herb Ellis and Barney Kessel did it, but with bass and drums as well, they were sailing in uncharted waters. I couldn't wait to hear the results.

As it turned out, I didn't have to. Space was made for an amp I hadn't noticed the day before, a Fender Twin Reverb, pre-CBS by the looks of it, top of the line. Somebody wasn't fooling around. Ernie found another metal folding chair and sat it slightly turned toward André's line of vision. When Lee opened her case, André whistled softly. "Wow. What an ax" was all he said. The oohs and aahs from Ernie, behind him, corroborated this opinion.

John D'Angelico was a New Yorker who between the early thirties and the mid-sixties had made over eleven hundred guitars, all by hand. With a double-cutaway body, this blond beauty was a knockout, unmistakably handmade by the master. The peg head's lavish inlay was a real work of art, beautiful enough to be prized by a collector, but, wonder of wonders, the instrument had somehow found its way into Lee Wilder's proud possession. "My dad used to have a music store in New Jersey," she said a little apologetically. "One night a couple of years ago, I was playing at the Blue Note and my old man came in with this case and set it up on the bandstand. I couldn't believe it."

"Let's plug her in," André said. "Let's not waste a moment of this—I could wake up any minute now."

In no time, both guitarists had tuned up and with only a couple of adjustments of volume and tone had started playing together as naturally as if they'd been doing it ever since kindergarten. Ernie and Al waited and watched along with me, allowing them to find their sound without the muddying effect of other instruments. They fooled around with Bill Evans's arrangement of "My Romance"—interesting, I thought, that they'd start with something by a pianist—and went directly into "Everytime We Say Goodbye," without any signals between them that I could detect. From there, they swung hard on "I Can't Give You Anything but Love," somehow managing to inject a little humor into the old standard. When they stopped, both were laughing with glee. "C'mon, boys, you better get in here while there's still some room for you," André said.

Al picked up his brushes and did a little practice swipe across his drums. "Ooh-wee," he said, "Lord, let me find that groove just one more time."

Well, the Lord was certainly with them that day, or something certainly was. I stopped bothering to scribble and, stretching out on the couch with my eyes closed, went into the kind of reverie I used to think could be achieved only with the aid of chemical interference. These two musicians were born to play together, and Ernie and Al instinctively knew how to buoy them up, embellishing where necessary, playing down when the guitarists needed more space for chord and melody. When the music ended, I didn't know how much time had passed and cared even less. I had been brought close to the ultimate of what music can offer.

When everyone had helped themselves to cold drinks— beer for all but André, who drank iced tea—I stepped over to the window for a Gitane, not wanting to be obnoxious with the smoke. But Lee Wilder's eyes had lit up when she saw the cigarettes and she asked whether I'd mind some company.

We smoked in silence at first, after having assured each other that we very rarely smoked. "How'd you get into playing jazz?" I asked. "You don't see that many women."

"And that ain't by accident," she said. "I started out playing blues and R&B, stuff I'd hear late at night on the radio. Then I heard Wes Montgomery and it was all over. I spent two years driving myself crazy, then decided to try to get into the Berklee College of Music and really study the guitar. I gigged around Boston some while I was in school, but it was hard to be accepted most places."

"Women were looked down upon?"

She nodded. "Down enough to be invisible. Some of the older players let me know in no uncertain terms what they thought women were meant for. I'd show up at jam sessions and slowly, one by one, every man on the bandstand would get up and leave." She looked at me with her piercing brown eyes.

"You're a woman in jazz, you'd better have a strong ego. And even then . . ." She broke off, musing.

"How about now?" I asked. "Is it any better with the younger guys?"

She shrugged. "A bit, I guess, but it's still a challenge at times. Well, there are guys like these here"—she gestured into the room—"who're regular princes. But I could use a few more like them. I still get drummers who automatically assume I don't have good time, who condescend and hold back until I prove something to them. But it gets tiring. All I ever wanted to do was to play the music."

I nodded and ground out my cigarette. "I used to play guitar in a rock band, and when we'd show up at a gig, people would assume I was the 'chick singer.' I hated it. So how'd you know André?"

Her face lit up again now. "He's a hero of mine. When I first heard him, I'd never even thought of playing like that. He's one of the few true originals, the best. We met a couple of times in Toronto and had this idea of doing something together someday. When I was invited to appear at the festival and heard André would be here as well, I got this flash—we'd never find a more receptive audience for this little experiment, and besides, it's the perfect opportunity for a real jazz experience, right there on the edge." She nodded to herself. "On the dangerous edge, where I like it," she said. "That's what it's supposed to be about."

Suddenly, I was sorry I *wasn't* writing about this for a real jazz magazine. I felt ashamed I'd had to lie to this wonderful woman, who was a rare find and my kind of beauty—one whose strength of character and heart were what gave her such considerable presence.

Oh well, I told myself, it's not like you haven't lied before, and you will again. Just enjoy the moment. And with that piece of sage advice, I smiled to my companion and stood up from my windowsill. "Could I get you another beer?" I asked. Actually, I'd do anything for this woman, other than voluntarily leave this room. Something told me that the best part of the Montreal Jazz Festival was happening right here and now, offstage, in a loft high above The Main, for only the delivery vans and street hawkers to hear.

---

Things being the way they were, I didn't get back to Raymond's couch until close to four A.M., so exhausted I fell into a dead sleep before I'd even had a chance to go over my day. I'd made arrangements with the band to show up a little later the next morning so Raymond and I could actually see each other in the flesh. After a relaxed breakfast of pâté and baguette and a bit of a chat with my friend, I headed over to St-Laurent, ready for another day of music and lolling about.

When I entered the loft, the tension in the room was crackling and popping like a good Southern thunderstorm. André sat in a corner by himself, smoking and rubbing his forehead, his eyes focused somewhere in the distance. Ernie and Al were talking in the hushed tones usually reserved for a sickroom.

Since André hadn't looked up when I'd come into the room, I headed over to the other two men. "What goes?" I asked. "Something happen?"

Ernie nodded. "André got a phone call early this morning that set him off. He wouldn't say anything about it, but obviously it wasn't good news."

I turned to Al. "You hear anything? Who answered the phone?"

"He did." He gestured toward André. "Most of the calls have been for him anyway, so it's not like we raced him for it. I'd been asleep, actually."

"You didn't catch any of the conversation?"

"Nope. It takes me a while to wake up."

I decided to face whatever it was head-on. Accepting a cup of coffee from Ernie, I walked over to André and sat down beside him. "Hey, it can't be this bad," I said by way of a greeting.

"That's what you think," he answered glumly.

"Is there something I can do? Remember, I'm here to make things easier for you. If someone's bothering you, I need to know it now."

André sighed heavily. He didn't say anything for a few minutes, appearing to be lost in thought, but when I didn't move away from him, he gradually began to come back from whatever dark room he'd been residing in. "Look," he said now. "I can't tell you everything because I don't know for sure. But I'd like you to make sure no one gets in to see me I didn't invite. Can you do that much for me? It's all I really need."

I nodded impatiently. "Of course I can do that, André, if you give me a list of who you've invited. That's easy. But I don't understand why you can't be up-front with me. It would make it one helluva lot easier to know who I'm supposed to be protecting you from." My own frustration was threatening to boil over; he'd never once been able to come completely clean with me—the man was impossible, not to mention stubborn.

I took some deep breaths, calming myself before I spoke again, slowly, as if to a three-year-old. "André, you're tying my hands here. I'm good at my job, but I need information. What you're asking me to do would be tantamount to working with a blindfold."

I could see from the expression on his face that I'd finally gotten through to him, but I realized, with a steadily rising sense of alarm, that my offer had just been refused. "I'll get you that list," he said, getting up. "That's the only way it can be right now."

Damn it to hell! I thought, looking around me for somebody to fight. Both Al and Ernie had sat down in front of their instruments, probably wisely, given the moods of their other two companions. André handed me a piece of paper with six names on it; one of them was Lee Wilder's. She arrived soon after that and the sounds of music started filling up the space inside the loft again, driving out whatever ruinous ghosts had inhabited it only moments before.

With the door opened so I could answer the phone if it should ring, I took a seat in the hallway just outside, with the band in clear sight. The door that led to the street level was in my direct line of vision as well, down two steep flights of stairs. Any outside surveillance I needed to do could be done from the café across the street.

Okay, I said to myself, you've got your plan, Lillian. Just show 'em your dogged side. Meanwhile, Al Sandberg's eyes were closed, his face turned heavenward in ecstasy, as Lee Wilder's solo on " 'Round Midnight" redefined the song's very intention. André comped for her, lost in concentration, supplying the kind of backup that many musicians never live to see. Then they traded places and, using all four fingers to pluck, André started his solo softly, then worked around the melody, weaving in and out of it without boundaries or doubt. As I leaned in to watch him, I saw him work the whole guitar neck, more pianist than guitar player, alternating effortlessly between fretted notes, harmonics, and chords. His sound reminded me of something—Yeah, I realized, incredulously, he sounds like he's playing the harp.

Once again, time stood still while music was being made. I stayed, glued to my seat, with one eye on the band and one eye peeled to the downstairs entrance. If I was all there was between André and trouble, then I would give it 200 percent.

109

I'd missed out on Charlie Parker, Coltrane, and Miles; I'd missed out on Rahsaan Roland Kirk, Billie Holliday, and Mary Lou Williams; but André Ledoux was sitting right there in the next room, within reach, playing out his pain, turning it into the beauty of creation.

# CHAPTER ELEVEN

S o m e t i m e s
I like to joke that it's my job that has finely honed my already-suspicious nature; without getting into the chicken-versus-egg problem, let's just say that I have a built-in excuse to check things out and to check thoroughly. I spent the rest of the afternoon and early evening sitting on my stool in the hall and I took my job of screening André's visitors seriously, feeling forced into seeing everyone as a possible suspect. It didn't make me feel particularly good, or popular, but that's one of the many hazards of my line of work.

When dinnertime rolled around, we accepted Raymond's invitation to eat at Le Bayou Fumeux—there are few hard-and-fast rules in life, but when a chef offers to cook you a special meal, you accept. We walked over to Duluth, grateful to have an opportunity for some exercise after a long day of sitting. André appeared much more relaxed, joking with Al and Ernie, who razzed him back as only old friends can do. Lee and I held down the rear, talking quietly.

Duluth is a small street that runs eastward from Parc Jeanne-Mance at the foot of Mount Royal to Parc Lafontaine. In the early eighties, gentrification had struck and now it's hard to find a simple neighborhood business among all the chic eateries and boutiques that have taken over. When Raymond's father died, his mother had decided to give her son something at least to replace the acceptance he'd never received from his old man. When a Portuguese neighbor decided to give up his business and retire to the country, he'd sold the small building to Raymond, whose nest egg was just the right size, liking the idea of turning things over to someone who used to stop by for milk and eggs.

Tonight, the chef had gone all out. We started with small bowls of a delicate crab-and-oyster gumbo, moving on to plates of shrimp creole and honest-to-God crawfish pie, with a side of dirty rice, for which I had a special fondness. Raymond served us himself with a graciousness I particularly associated with well-raised Southerners, no matter where they actually resided. I wasn't disappointed. By the time we were hoggishly downing pieces of delicious pecan pie, Raymond had taken off his apron to sit with us. The strong chicory-laced coffee brought a perfect ending to a memorable meal.

André wrote something down on a piece of paper and handed it to Raymond. Raymond smiled when he saw what it was. "Comp tickets," he said to me. He reached across the table to shake André's hand. "Thanks, man. I love your music and I'd be honored to go, I really would."

"Just call these folks right away so nothing gets fucked up," André said, laughing a little. "I'm not the biggest name at the festival, so who knows? Maybe I'll have to pay my own way in."

This started a whole round of teasing, André cheerfully making himself the butt of most of the jokes. Lee Wilder joined in, a little shyly, I noticed. As I watched the banter of old friends and partners, I wondered whether Lee's position as a woman musician had excluded her somewhat from the camaraderie that even these nice men were able to take for granted.

Raymond's touch brought me out of my thoughts. "Whatcha doing after this?" he asked quietly.

"Tonight?"

"Yeah. Coming back to the flat with me or are you sticking with these guys?"

I'd been thinking about that. "I'm gonna stay outside the loft tonight, keep an eye on things."

"Want some company?"

Now there was an idea. I hadn't been looking forward to spending a night in the car by myself, stakeouts being the least-favorite part of my job. "It's really boring," I said. "We'd be sitting in the car drinking coffee while the rest of the world sleeps."

Raymond shrugged. "I get lots of sleep. The way I figure it, it's a golden opportunity to hang out a little—we still haven't gotten to spend much time together. Besides, I've always wondered what you private eyes do. Not only that but I have a great big thermos."

Now he'd done it. "And could we drink chicory coffee?"

He grinned. "My dear, please allow me to provide the java. And I don't suppose it would be appropriate for me to bring along a little cognac, would it? Just to keep us alert, of course."

"You Southern boys sure do know how to get to a girl," I said. "Okay. What if you grab the car and meet me in front of the loft. I'll walk everybody back, then you and I can get settled in."

He nodded. "My car's bigger. Want me to bring that instead?"

It was a good idea. Raymond drove a '73 Pontiac Le-Mans, which could easily have swamped a couple of apartments I'd lived in. We agreed to the details, then I rounded up the musicians for a leisurely stroll back to St-Laurent.

---

The Main had its own flavor at any time of the day, but a part of it seemed to belong to the night. When the stores shut down at six, the other Main came to life. At night, cars cruised

113

by slowly, looking for love or sex or a painkiller. Young men wandered in and out of the taverns and bars nearby. Occasionally, a couple would walk by fast, already on their way to someplace else, their conversation heated or excited or bored. Further down The Main, near Ste-Catherine, were the notorious sex clubs and dingy bars that catered to the darker side of the human experience. There, prostitutes congregated on street corners, and for a small gesture and a show of paper with the queen's picture on it, fantasy and reality sometimes merged. This was the stuff of nightmares to parents with a missing daughter or son, a place where an object of desire could quickly turn into human bait in the split second it took to light a crack pipe or snort a line or fill a needle.

From where Raymond and I sat in the Pontiac, we looked out on a sort of spillover area, where the men who cruised the night were hoping not to have to pay to fulfill their dreams. Some were closet cases wishing for solace in the dark and others were potential gay-bashers or rapists, but most were probably just lonely. At three A.M., a van stopped to discharge its passengers—a group of immigrant women in black, most likely coming from their under-the-table job in a nearby sweatshop; we were also on the fringes of the garment district. The women's talk was fast and animated in spite of the lateness of the hour. They knew their world, and their place in it was solid and sure.

I dozed off sometime between five and six A.M. and awoke around seven, feeling sore and cranky. Raymond slept in the backseat, curled up like a little child on a car trip, huddled in his leather jacket. Stifling an urge to poke him awake, I got out of the car and walked up and down the block a couple of times, hoping to stretch out my sore spots. By the time I returned with some sweet rolls and orange juice, Raymond was sitting up, looking dazed and bleary-eyed. "So much for the romance of your job," he growled. "I'd rather be a CPA."

"No you wouldn't," I said. "You'd miss the glamour."

With a snort of disdain, he climbed over the seat and helped himself to a roll. While we were eating, I noticed a young woman walking toward the entrance to the loft. She had a determined gait and until the last second appeared ready to jerk open the door and go inside. But then she seemed to lose her resolve and, lighting up a smoke, stood there nervously puffing for a couple of minutes, looking up and down the street as if it held her answers.

She was young and well dressed, maybe nineteen or twenty, with apple cheeks and straight dark hair held away from her face by a couple of lilac barettes. When she abruptly turned and walked away, I was about to jump out of the car and follow her on foot, but she opened the door of a battered Toyota and climbed in. I started up the Pontiac and fell in behind her.

It didn't take me long to realize we weren't going any place in particular. She followed St-Laurent as far as Bernard where she took a left and meandered around the streets of Outremont, pausing once or twice at a stop sign as if to decide whether to turn right or left. Outremont was an old, affluent French neighborhood with large trees and well-cared-for stone buildings for both single families and apartment dwellers. Stop signs at almost every block slowed traffic down, making it safe for kids and old people. A few early-morning strollers and joggers headed for the parks that dotted the area, giving it a humane, relaxed appearance.

But then the woman made a series of left turns that, I soon realized, were taking us back toward The Main. I dropped back a little, using the early traffic as a buffer. "Do you think she knows we're here?" Raymond asked. "Is she doing this for our benefit?"

I shook my head. "I doubt it. She's going too slow."

She drove south as far as Sherbrooke before hooking a left onto St-Laurent. Nearing the loft, the vehicle slowed once again and she signaled before a likely parking space.

"What's she working herself up to?" I said. I didn't like it. André had been scared by someone and I knew that stalkers came in all sexes and stripes.

I used the Pontiac's power steering to wedge the car into a tiny space across the street, feeling my gut tense up with excitement—or dread. I glanced over at Raymond briefly. "Stay here and be my witness," I said. "I'm gonna check this babe out."

I jumped out of the car and wincing at the stiffness in my legs, bounded across the street, taking momentary cover behind a double-parked delivery van. This time the woman didn't hesitate, flinging the door open and disappearing inside, with me only a few paces behind. She heard me coming halfway up the first flight of stairs and turned around, confusion and panic on her face. Stiff or not, I used her hesitation to gain some speed and ran directly toward her like a bull on stampede. I stopped only when my face was a couple of inches from hers.

"What are you doing here?" I panted. "Who are you?"

"I'm . . . I'm . . ." She looked about ready to cry. "I just wanted to see him," she said.

"See who? What do you want?"

Abruptly all the starch left her and her body seemed to collapse. I reached out to break her fall, but she just plopped down on the nearest step, her head on her knees. The remainder of my adrenaline rush took a hike and I gratefully sat down myself, frowning at the young girl who sobbed into her lap, as if she was sobbing out the whole of her young existence.

This time, I reached out a comforting hand. "Who are you?" I asked again.

She kept right on crying for a couple more minutes, then looked up at me with red-rimmed, swollen eyes. "You keep it up, you're gonna make me bawl, too," I said. "Now, who are

116

you?" I couldn't exactly call this communication—it was more like talking to myself in front of a witness.

"I'm his daughter," she said, starting to cry again.

I sat up. "Whose daughter?"

"André Ledoux's!" she replied, and her words set off a whole new set of waterworks. I sat there dumbly, staring at a lovely young girl who, I suddenly realized, looked an awful lot like a certain guitarist who had been driving me nuts for the last few days.

I'll say one thing: Life's never dull for too long.

---

We sat there for a few minutes, the girl sniffling while I mulled things over. I rooted around in my shirt pocket for a Kleenex and handed it over.

"You got a name?" I asked.

"Lorraine. Lorraine Owens."

"Well, Lorraine Owens, will your father know you when he sees you? Or is this a little surprise?"

She frowned, and for a moment I was afraid I'd set her off again, but she held on to her control.

"He knows about me, but I haven't seen him since I was little." She took a deep breath. "He and my mom were real young when they had me and they broke up when I was three. I saw him only a couple of times after that." She looked down at the Kleenex she was strangling.

"And did you stay in touch?"

She shook her head. "My stepfather was jealous and my mom held some stuff against him, too, so he stopped coming. Then we moved. I guess he was pretty unhappy, too."

I nodded. He'd most likely buried his memories of those early years in one back alley or another.

"Can I see your ID?" I asked. "You look like him and you say he knows about you, but I've gotta do my job, okay?"

She reached into her bag and extracted her wallet. "It's not a very good picture, but it's me," she said, resigned.

I looked it over. Lorraine Owens was twenty-two years old and resided at 321 McDowell Road, Kitchener, Ontario. She was five feet five and weighed 125 pounds. She did not need glasses to drive. I handed it back.

"What brought you here just now? How'd you know where to find him?"

"I have a friend here who told me about the Jazz Festival and I asked if André was playing, like I was a fan or something. And he was. When I found out my father was going to be here, I asked my boss for a week off and he gave it to me. I'm crashing at my friend Rubin's apartment."

Once she started talking, she was quite good at it, I thought. "Could you wait in the café across the street while I talk to him? I mean, you don't look like any three-year-old and he might need a couple of minutes." I smiled, trying to soften the inference. André Ledoux had lost a whole lot of baggage through the years and I, for one, couldn't predict how he'd react to some of it popping back up a couple of days away from an important gig. She reluctantly got up, hanging onto the railing with one hand while she drummed up her courage once again. "What if he doesn't want to see me? What if he's mad I found him?"

"Then we'll start there and see what happens. But don't start thinking the worst, okay? Just give me a few minutes with him first."

She walked back down the stairs, a fashionably dressed young woman with the needs of a hurt three-year-old still inside her. Was I only imagining it or did people in their twenties take longer to grow up than they used to? I shook my head and approximated a sign of the cross before I knocked on André's door. I wasn't Catholic, but sometimes it's nice to have a prop, anyway.

Raymond and Al scrambled some eggs, while Ernie stuffed bread into a toaster oven. We were eating because we were hungry, but that was the simple part. We were swallowing our curiosity, as well. André and the girl had been at Café Vincente for over an hour.

To amuse myself further, I observed Raymond around Al and vice versa. Could it be that love was in bloom? Their chatter was certainly animated considering the time of day, and neither seemed likely to run out of something to say anytime soon.

I nudged Ernie, who still didn't look completely awake. "Did you know about this girl? Does his wife, for that matter?"

He nodded. "André always felt bad about leaving her, I think, but he wouldn't talk about it unless he was out of it, and I mean *way* out. But according to him, Irene knows. I got the feeling he was holding onto a shitload of guilt about the way he checked out on his daughter, but he couldn't figure out what to do about it, so he didn't do anything. Believe me, there have been lots of issues he's just never been able to deal with."

"Is there something that tells you he's gotten any better at it in the last few weeks?"

Ernie shrugged and gave me a sad look. "I keep hoping. He's got great stuff, if only he'd believe it. On the other hand, maybe she's just what he needs. He's been trying for a new start the past few months—maybe he just needs a little push in the right direction."

Breakfast was served and eaten. While we were drinking coffee, I heard a sound at the door and turned around as father and daughter walked in wearing identical shy smiles.

Maybe, I thought, help has just arrived. It was at least a start.

## CHAPTER TWELVE
■ ■ ■ ■ ■ ■ ■ ■ ■ ■ ■ ■ ■ ■ ■ ■

T h e
next couple of days were something out of an old dream for
me. The festival had started and the streets were filled with the
sounds of music. Musicians and fans rubbed elbows on the
streets as the crowds roamed excitedly from concert halls to
small cafés where the jazz was free. Some streets had roped-
off areas where musicians ranging all the way from amateur
to seasoned pro gave all they had to anyone who took the time
to stop and listen. St-Denis, the original home of the festival,
was mobbed with smiling people. There, a sound would grab
a walker's attention, so faint and subtle they would hesitate
before turning around to see its source. And in a doorway,
partially hidden, would be a young man selling his wares,
whispering close to someone's ear, "Hash . . . hash . . ."
drawing out the end of the word like the hiss of a snake.

André was flying high himself. His daughter's appearance had been the shot in the arm he had needed to find the
courage to walk into the spotlight, where he belonged. The
two had been inseparable since that first day, making up for
a lot of wasted years. I had had a couple of long talks with him
as well and his optimism about the future was beautiful to see.
Even Ernie was impressed, and he had known André the
longest and the best. The cloud that André Ledoux had lived
under for most of his adult life had finally lifted, leaving in its
place a sunny sky.

120

One other thing happened that had freed me up to enjoy this special time in the city: I'd been fired. André had come to me the day after his daughter had shown up and said that the troubles he'd been having were "all fixed," and he didn't need me to guard him anymore. I'd been skeptical and annoyed at being bounced around like a goofy beach ball and I had harangued and harassed him, acting like an all-around pain in the ass. I made Ernie sit in with us while we discussed this weird business and finally was forced to take André at his word: He didn't want a guard dog. I convinced him to let my journalist cover stay, though, and to let me hang around until the festival was over. I didn't feel good about leaving him entirely on his own, although if I'd been able to make the assessment myself, using all the information André'd denied me all along, I would have, I was sure. Now, I could kick back, enjoy myself a bit, and still be within safe range should my ex-client need me.

But the music! Archie Shepp wailed on his saxophone for a full two hours that first night of the festival. Tall and good-looking, his power and strength were equaled only by the great amount of feeling and love he put into his playing. When he did the recitation for "Mama Rose," his hymn to his grandmother, my flesh tingled with goose bumps. I closed my eyes for a few minutes and drifted off into a quiet place I didn't visit often enough.

Thanks to André, who turned out to be as big a fan as any of us, we were able to see as many concerts as time would allow. Having spent those long days in rehearsal early on, the musicians were now free to use their comp tickets and enjoy everything the festival had to offer, and I tagged along as their journalist friend. And what a banquet it was!

Sheila Jordan, enough warmth radiating from her to embrace a large audience, sang with humor and style, taking huge risks to make her music the very essence of what jazz should be: bold and subtle at the same time. She was quick with a laugh or a joke, but the seriousness of her intent was never lost, nor were the musical intimations of the struggle in which her special talents had been honed. Although she frequently liked to work with solo bass accompaniment, here she was featured with a full band—sax, stand-up bass, piano, and drums. The piano player was a slender blonde in her forties with an amazing ability to move from tenderness to intense swinging in less than a heartbeat. She played with her head down, swaying slightly with the beat, catching every nuance Sheila threw her way, reinterpreting the sound and volleying it back like a rich echo of the original.

There was local talent to burn, as well—among them, the guitarist Sonny Greenwich, who played with a tone nearly hornlike, and Lorraine Desmarais, a Québec pianist and composer whose self-described acoustic fusion brought us to our feet in awe and delight. Then there were accordian players from Louisiana and Paris and musicians from the continent of Africa, stretching and reaching to bring the audience updated versions of music and rhythms as old as the earth itself.

By Sunday afternoon, the excitement in the air was as potent as the storm preceding a Texas tornado. Word had gotten around about André and Lee Wilder and the phone in the loft hadn't stopped ringing in days. Responding to their billing as the "André Ledoux Trio, with Special Guest Lee Wilder," faithful fans of both had gathered, anticipating great enjoyment from what seemed a perfect showcase for two talents who had yet to taste the full measure of wordly success each so richly deserved. The concert had been sold out since Saturday morning and the buzz going around was that people had already lined up outside the theater in the wild hope that there would be standing room.

After the sound check, we sneaked out through the stage entrance for a light meal at a Thai restaurant on St-Denis, near Duluth. Though the curry was good, all but Al were too revved up to do it justice. Even Lee, usually reserved and restrained, was giddy with exhilaration. André, whom I had seen most often as a shy, moody man, played the clown for his friends now, sneaking his daughter looks from time to time, making a point of catching her eye when he was at his funniest. Not that it was hard to get her attention—Lorraine, having found her father, was sticking to him like burrs to a big black dog.

Time got away from me that afternoon as it seldom does. Before I knew it, I was sitting between Raymond and Lorraine at the Théâtre Saint-Denis, nervously rolling and unrolling my program, waiting for the curtain to go up. When the house lights went down and the four musicians were introduced, a deafening cheer broke out. In those moments, André Ledoux, Franco-American musical genius, became Québec's long-lost son. He beamed as the thunderous homage of so many unknown compatriots rolled up to the stage. Shouting their fervent bravos, they thanked him for having finally come to share his magic with them. They were claiming him forever. It was so moving that my eyes teared up and I hardly heard the other introductions.

In short order, magic did take over the theater. André and Lee switched in and out of each other's musical lines as if they were but one player, each in turn holding back until the other left open a space needing to be filled in the sacred flow, the song. Then, without the smallest hesitation, the tune would shift and André would solo while Lee comped for him or he for her. Al played with his eyes closed much of the time, using percussion instruments I had never even heard of to add texture and exotic coloring to the material, growling happily in his trademark expression of immeasurable joy. Ernie West was brilliant, too, that night. His left hand flew deftly up and down the neck of the bass, while his right tenderly bowed or plucked the strings. He was swinging hard.

The crowd went wild, roaring its approval. Most of the

audience had gotten to its feet early on and had never sat down again. There was only one moment without music, cheering, or clapping and it was the one chosen by André to speak. Not one to talk much onstage, this time he stood and approached the mike, waiting for the crowd to calm down.

"*Merci, Montréal, de nous avoir si bien reçus.*" "Thank you, Montreal, for welcoming us this way," he said softly in French. That drove his fans crazy, of course, and for a moment the clapping and bravos surged again. When it was quieter, he continued: "I've waited a long time to find my way, as many of you in the audience tonight already know. My friends here on this stage with me deserve a lot of credit for helping keep me alive to play this music." Again there was a roar of appreciation from the crowd and both Ernie and Al, looking touched, took little bows and waved to the audience.

"I'm very proud to have had the opportunity to play tonight with one of the finest guitarists to grace the world of jazz. It's not often that musicians, or anyone else, find this kind of intimacy and communication anywhere and, believe me, that's what it takes." He turned so he faced her a bit when he said, "Thank you, Lee Wilder, from the bottom of my heart." Lee stood and cradling her blond guitar, bowed deeply from the waist toward André, as she had on that first day.

"Now I would like to dedicate this song to my daughter, Lorraine, who's here in the audience tonight. We haven't had much time together so far, but I intend to see that we do from now on. The song is called 'Softly, As in a Summer Sunrise'—Lorraine, honey, this is for you."

Then he sat down and began to play, at first alone, then, after a bit, indicating to Lee that she should join in. Al and Ernie hung back until the chorus came up again and then slipped in quietly. Lorraine had grabbed one of my hands and Raymond clutched the other. I doubt there was a dry eye in the house; there certainly wasn't where we sat.

The group played three encores and the cheers and clapping continued long after the musicians abandoned the stage. Then the audience lit matches and cigarette lighters and, holding them high over their heads, gave a final, silent tribute to the musicians who had touched their hearts and minds so deeply that evening.

The three of us ran backstage like the fans we were and there was much hugging and backslapping for the next hour or so. We'd had to wade through at least a dozen journalists and critics, and I was betting that when news of this extraordinary performance got out to the big newspapers and magazines, all four musicians would be in for a whole new appraisal from the music industry that had paid them such scant attention over the years. It looked as if the good times were on their way.

We made plans to celebrate at Le Bayou Fumeux, which was closed to the public on Sundays. Raymond had stocked a case of champagne and had prepared some food, as well. After Raymond told them to bring along anyone they wanted, he and I left the musicians to say good-bye to their friends and fans. We would meet in an hour.

As I got ready to leave, André rushed over and we exchanged a kiss and a long hug. "Ya done good," I whispered into his ear. He beamed back at me, tears in his eyes.

# CHAPTER THIRTEEN

R aymond
and I had all but floated around the restaurant as we set out
the platters of Cajun delicacies with which we would greet our
conquering heroes. We chattered as gaily as a flock of barn
swallows, unable and unwilling to come down from the natu-
ral high the evening's musical experience had left us with.
The bottles of champagne—not the cheap stuff, either—were
sitting on ice and the tables were elegantly laid out with flower
centerpieces. Meanwhile, Raymond and I cracked open a bottle of champagne, just to test it, of course, and we each lit up
a Gitane for the same reason. In minutes, the place would be
swamped. This was our private celebration, two old friends
sharing something new.

Then people started arriving in twos and threes. Ernie
was as outgoing as I'd ever seen him, his handsome face
relaxed and open. He stuck close to Lee Wilder, I noticed,
never missing an opportunity for eye contact or to smile at
something she'd said. When had this happened? I thought. I
must have been blind.

It was only after having noticed Lorraine checking her
watch a couple of times that it dawned on me the main guest
of honor was still missing. Lorraine had been one of the first
to arrive, saying that André had had something to do and
would be along soon—"probably before the champagne was
uncorked." I'd figured he was doing an interview—some of

126

the press was European and their time in the city might be limited—and hadn't thought about it twice. But when I checked my own watch, I realized André was two hours late for his own party.

When he hadn't showed up at midnight, I was wild with worry. André had waited too long for a celebration such as this and I couldn't believe he would willingly duck out on his own party. Lorraine's face mirrored my own growing anxiety as she glanced at her watch every couple of minutes. I made my way over to her through the crowd.

"Lorraine, what did André say exactly? Did he tell you where he was going?"

She shook her head. "He just said that he had to take care of something and then he'd be over. I didn't want to leave him, so I asked if I could come along, but he said no."

I frowned. "How did he say it, exactly? Can you remember?"

She thought for a moment. "He said he needed to go by himself but not to worry, that everything was going to be okay from now on. He'd been on the phone for a minute right before that."

"Did he seem upset?"

She shook her head. "He seemed relieved, kind of. He said we were finally going to be a family and not to worry about a thing."

I don't know about anyone else, but when somebody tells me not to worry, it usually hits my stomach like a hot pastrami sandwich at three in the morning. I checked with Ernie and Al, who, like me, were realizing all was not right in Eden. Then I spoke briefly with Raymond before slipping out the back way. I'd found the man twice already—what was one more time?

I spent the next three hours driving all over the city. First I tried the loft, then went back to the theater, which was dark and locked up tight. I hit all the late-night jazz clubs I could think of, from the posh ones in Old Montreal to places like Le Soleil Levant, which featured blues, jazz, and African music. There were crowds everywhere, people bopping from one musical event to the other, and the lateness of the hour didn't appear to impress anyone much. No one had seen André Ledoux.

I took to driving around the congested downtown streets. Festivalgoers, high on music, had spilled over into bars, pubs, and restaurants that had nothing to do with jazz, unable and unwilling to unwind and call it a night. My own enthusiasm was long gone, replaced by feelings of panic and guilt. Why had I let him slough off my help? If anything happened to him, it would be my fault.

Ben's Deli was brightly lighted and I peered inside, in search of a familiar face. He wasn't there. I roamed up St-Catherine's, past joints called La Cave du Sexe, Club Sexy Lady, and something called Pussy Corps—Private Dancer. I didn't expect to find André there, either, but it was better than doing nothing. I stopped three times to call Raymond, who still hadn't heard anything. He was going back to the apartment, he said, and would stay by the phone. The party was over.

I thought about going to the cops but could imagine their amusement at reporting a famous jazz musician missing just because he was a few hours late to a party. They wouldn't be of any help, and if he showed up later, at least I could save André that embarrassment. Finally, with dawn just an hour away, I was exhausted. No longer able to keep my eyelids open, I was fast becoming a hazard on the streets. Headed up St-Laurent one last time, I made the turns that would take me to de Bullion. Now I was blocking out everything except the vision of Raymond's comfortable sofa and my intense desire for a few hours of sleep.

Raymond had hit the sack himself. His note told me that André still hadn't turned up and that Lorraine, sick with worry, had finally been convinced to go back to her friend's apartment for the night. I crashed as soon as I hit the pillow and didn't dream at all.

At eight A.M., the phone woke us up. It was Ernie West. An employee at the exclusive Hôtel Bienvenue downtown had discovered a fully clothed body lying at the bottom of the heated rooftop pool at six-thirty A.M. The Montreal cops, upon finding a laminated Jazz Festival ID in the man's suit pocket, had put in a couple of calls to determine whom to notify locally. Ernie told me this, then hung up before I could reply.

I stood with my mouth open, all my worst fears closing in on me as I tried to absorb the news. André Ledoux would play no more. The music had stopped.

I sank down to the couch and bawled like a baby.

---

Who says you must know someone intimately and long to feel profound grief? The next couple of hours were uncontrollably lost to tears and self-recrimination, but then with Raymond's help I rallied enough to do the tasks I knew were mine and mine alone to do. I went over to the loft and spoke with Ernie, whose eyes were glazed and haunted, and with Al, who sat in utter stillness in a chair in front of a window facing the street. They had had to identify the body of their friend only an hour before. Death had entered the loft quietly, like a burglar, and had emptied it of all music and joy.

From there, I put in a phone call to Detective Luc Rivard. I offered to go down to the station, but he said he'd just as soon meet me at the loft—he had some more questions for the guys, anyway—and to stay put until he arrived. That wasn't hard—I'd been knocked out flat by a sucker punch and I was still reeling. I took up residence on the chrome-and-leather sofa and let the time float by in silence.

Detective Rivard arrived forty minutes later, a huge, powerful-looking man dressed casually in an open-necked blue shirt and a cream-colored jacket. His size and physicality made me think of a professional football or hockey player, but it also looked good on a cop, intimidating as hell. He eyed me neutrally as we talked, giving nothing away, probing politely but insistently, and found out in minutes what it had taken me weeks to come up with. Of course, I was telling the facts as I knew them—André had always given me an edited version. I still didn't know how much of what he'd told me was the truth and now maybe I never would.

At the very least, I intended to know the facts surrounding the man's death. "Did André Ledoux die from drowning? Was there evidence to confirm that?"

The detective looked at me sharply. Cops weren't known for sharing information or for feeling the need to. "There will be an autopsy later today, after his wife has been notified. Then we will know for sure."

Why couldn't he have just said yes? Was there more?

But he broke into my thoughts. "Madame, one more question, please, and then I'll be going, for now." He looked at me and I nodded. "Why did you not leave, after Monsieur Ledoux fired you? What were you thinking of?"

I thought about that for a minute. Maybe my senses had been dulled by the violence of my last case and maybe I should have taken a couple more months off before getting involved in anything serious again. That was what I'd been trying to do before Ernie West's plea for help had broken into my defenses and had caused me to jump back into the fray, unarmed in a sense.

Detective Rivard was still looking at me with sharp cop's eyes that missed nothing. I hugged myself, shivering in the July heat, and finally shrugged. "I don't know," I said. "Something wasn't right, but I didn't know what it was. Just a gut feeling."

He stared at me for a few seconds, then nodded slightly, closing his notebook before dropping it into a jacket pocket.

"It's never just a gut feeling, is it?" he said now, getting to his feet. "Let the police take care of everything from now on, Madame Ritchie. We'll find out what happened for you."

I assured him I would stay out of his way and would be available for any other questions he might have. In a certain sense, I wasn't lying—I *did* intend to stay out of his way. But I had questions of my own that would need to be answered if I was ever to sleep soundly again.

———————

I found Lorraine at her friend's second-floor flat on Waverly. Here, Hassid boys walked along the street with their fathers, dressed alike in black outfits and hats, long locks of hair on either side of their faces. The conservatively dressed girls and women walked behind, chatting with one another and avoiding eye contact with passersby.

Here, too, people tended to congregate on the balconies and elegantly shaped exterior staircases unique to this city. Most of the old homes had been converted to apartments and the neighborhood's ethnic mix was a microcosm of modern Montreal. Asian children rode up and down the sidewalks on bikes while their parents kept a protective eye. Many of the corner stores were owned and operated by Greeks or Italians, Hassids or Israelis, who also lived nearby. Each long block was full of children absorbed in the games they were playing. The older kids had loudly taken over the street itself, throwing a ball back and forth and scattering every time someone needed to drive through. Vehicles were squeezed so tightly into parking spaces that they resembled the cars of a skinny, jumbled-up train.

Lorraine answered the door herself, eyes almost swollen shut from crying. She let me in, then went back to her chair by the window, soggy Kleenex littering the area around it like dead petals off a flower. I sat down near her and tried to think of something helpful to say. There wasn't anything, of course. I ended up asking her for a drink of water instead.

"Lorraine, I'm so sorry," I said, my voice beginning to waver. "I don't know what happened, but we'll find out."

She gave me a flat look, cold and gone. Shock, I thought. "He always left me," she said.

"Not by choice, he didn't. Not this time. He loved you—everyone could see it."

Her chin started quivering and soon she was sobbing from her gut, much as I had done after my early-morning phone call. Then Raymond, a man who had lost many friends to AIDS, had comforted me. I'd been strengthened by his ability to handle death from the hot center of grief. I went over to Lorraine now and knelt down by her chair, taking her limp, damp form into my arms. I held her there firmly, rocking her a little while she cried. When my shoulder was damp with her tears, she sat up a little and I slipped onto a small stool next to her chair, within reach. "It's not fair," she said, sniffling.

"No, baby, it's not," I said. "It never is—that's the bitch of it."

"Do you know what happened to my father? Was he pushed in, or did he fall?"

It was one of the key questions, but so far I didn't have the answer. "They'll find out a little later today, I think. Meanwhile, you've got to take good care of yourself." I looked around. "Is your friend here? You're not all alone, are you?"

"He's gone out to get me something for my headache and something to eat. He knew you were coming, so he thought it would be all right."

"Good. I'll stay here until he gets back." There was something else. I hated to mention it. "Lorraine, does your mother know where you are? You might call her, in case she hears something on the news."

"I'll call her later. Rubin talked to her a little while ago."

I nodded. "Okay. That's good."

Just then, the front door opened and a serious-looking young man entered. He craned his neck to see around the entranceway, frowning slightly with concern when he saw us in the corner. I got up. "Lil Ritchie," I said, extending a hand, which he shook firmly. "I'm Rubin Truslow. I'm glad you could come over."

"I'm glad, too." He was slender and fine-boned, with the intelligent face of a scholar. His straight dark hair fell down toward his eyes, and I noticed him mechanically push it out of his face with a much-practiced gesture. "Could I offer you something?" he asked. "Some coffee or tea?"

I got to my feet. "No thanks, Rubin. I need to get going, actually. I'll just take my glass back into the kitchen." I looked at him pointedly, hoping he'd get the message and follow me. Thankfully, Lorraine wasn't paying all that much attention.

He took the hint and I dawdled at the sink, trying to decide what to ask him. "You've known Lorraine awhile?" I finally said.

"Since we were in college together, back in London, Ontario. Now I'm in graduate school at McGill, but we've always stayed in touch."

I figured I might as well be direct. "Are you two seriously involved?"

He smiled a little and shook his head. "We're friends. I'm gay and Lorraine was one of the first friends I made in school. We've been close ever since."

I thought about that for a moment. "Stay with her today, Rubin, will you? She's pretty shaky and we don't even know all the facts of her father's death yet. I wouldn't want to think of her having too much time alone right now."

"I don't have anywhere to go for the rest of the day, and I can free tomorrow up, too, if necessary. I'll take care of her," he said.

I believed him. I told Lorraine I'd be in touch, said

good-bye, and walked back down the stairs to my car. I sat there for a good twenty minutes with my eyes shut, listening to the children's laughter and shouts. But they failed to make me feel any better.

# CHAPTER FOURTEEN

I f

Monday had seemed like a long, bad dream, then the night was something straight out of Dante's Inferno. I had waited around the loft with the guys the rest of the afternoon, in vain as it turned out; the autopsy wouldn't be performed until the next morning, for some undisclosed reason. Feeling suddenly drained of all emotion and energy, I took my leave and skulked back to Raymond's, tired of the looks on the faces of everyone I saw. When I caught a glimpse of myself in the bathroom mirror, I knew what they had seen. Raymond threw me worried glances but knew to keep his distance.

Disgusted, I curled up on the couch, managing to sleep through the evening and part of the night. When I woke up at three A.M., it was with a pounding heart and an aching gut. My nightmare had taken me into the dark world of my own psyche, where André Ledoux had hovered in space and fallen. In a sweat, I sat up and rubbed my eyes, not bothering to turn on the lights.

After a while, I threw on my jeans and a T-shirt and, closing the door quietly behind me, stepped outside into the night. The air was muggy and still, the streets empty. With nothing particular in mind, I walked slowly down the rickety staircase, sitting for a few minutes on the bottom step while I tied my shoes. Then I headed up de Bullion and took a left onto Duluth, crossing St-Laurent against the light, then St-

Urbain. When I reached Parc Jeanne-Mance, I walked on the grass for a while, enjoying the soft feel of it and taking comfort in the dignified old row houses facing the park on L'Esplanade, like a New France version of Henry James's Washington Square. But on this particular street there was no square, no facing rows of houses to constrict the occupants' view—just a generous expanse of trees and green grass, blending across Park Avenue with the splendor of Mount Royal.

I walked across the soccer field, resting my eyes on the huge old trees, mostly maples, that separated the field from the tennis courts. Drawn toward them, I leaned against the largest tree for a few minutes, gazing out at nothing. I stood hidden in the shadows now, knowing that if someone else wandered into the park, I would see them long before they saw me, if they saw me at all. Something uncomfortable passed over me then and I turned from it quickly with a shudder and wandered over to the tennis courts, where I weaved my fingers loosely through the chain-link fence and rested my forehead on its cool, uneven surface. I stayed like that for what seemed like a long time.

When I let myself back into the apartment, it was still, with only the sounds of Raymond's light snoring to remind me I wasn't alone. I took off my shoes and rolled what my Texan friends like to call a New York joint—meaning it's skimpy—and tiptoed out to the back balcony, which overlooked the unused courtyard below. I leaned against the wooden railing, smoking the joint until it burned my fingers. I followed that with a Gitane and a glass of wine.

André's face floated out there somewhere, as it had all night. It wasn't accusing me of not helping him, but it didn't have to—I was doing that well enough myself. Other faces followed: Lorraine's, Lucie Pinkham's, and, oh God, I thought then, his aunt Eulalie. What's she going to do? Startling myself, I didn't realize I'd dropped the glass until I heard it shatter against a rock in the courtyard.

I shook my head and, feeling weak in the knees, plopped down on the old Volkswagen seat that served as a balcony chair. Tomorrow, I'd hear the results of the autopsy and not until then would I know how much I had failed the man whose music and gently tragic self had so touched my soul. Until then, I would watch the sun come up without him, the biggest insult of all.

———————

The detective, Rivard, called early in the morning to say he would be by to see me sometime in the next couple of hours. Again I offered to go down to the station to talk to him, and again he politely declined. Okay, I thought, he's got his reasons. I would be here.

Raymond hung around for a while, trying to get me to eat something, and finally, to shut him up, I swallowed some toast and marmalade. Then we sat together quietly and drank our second cups of coffee. I noticed him looking at me and I looked back, suddenly wondering just when he had gone from the young boy I had known to this thin, pared-down adult. "It's not your fault," he said. "You did the best you could."

I didn't say anything back.

"Just remember that someday you'll look back and this will all be behind you."

"I wonder if it ever will be," I said.

Raymond scooted his chair over and put his arm around my shoulder and we sat like that, without talking, for a few minutes. Then he got up, walked over to the stereo, and put on an old Leonard Cohen album that contained many of the songs we had loved and played in our youth. "It's still good, isn't it?" he said.

It was very good.

After Raymond went to work, I walked over to the *dépanneur* at the end of the block to get another pack of Gitanes. I was turning into quite the little smoker. Sitting behind the counter were two women, one elderly, dressed in black and missing some front teeth, and the other, young and vibrant, a Mediterranean beauty. A man stacked up cans of vegetables, whistling an unfamiliar melody while he worked. When I paid, the older of the women said something to me in Portuguese.

The young woman said, "Don't you mind my mother. She wants to know if you live in the neighborhood. If you do, she'll show you pictures of her farm in the country."

I smiled at the old lady and told her I did not live in the neighborhood but that sometimes I wished I did. The daughter translated and the old woman nodded solemnly and patted my hand. She asked me, through the daughter, if I had children, and when I said no, she shook her head sadly and said something else, which didn't really need a translator. She looked like a good old woman and I was sorry to disappoint her.

When I got back to the apartment, I thought about calling Ernie but couldn't quite face it. Maybe after Detective Rivard leaves, I thought to myself. Then I poured myself another cup of coffee, lit up a fresh Gitane, and waited.

He arrived within twenty minutes, looking worn-out, with eyes that craved sleep. When I offered him a seat on the couch, he sat down gratefully, pulling a bit at his linen jacket, as if he was hot inside it. I knew it was hiding his shoulder holster, so I didn't comment other than to ask him whether he would like some water before we talked.

He drank the water and set the glass down carefully on Raymond's low table. "You have the results of the autopsy," I said.

He looked at me sharply, then nodded. "I thought you

would be interested to know what happened to your client," he said in his gruff smoker's voice.

"Was he murdered?"

"*Oui, madame.* No doubt about it." He took out his notebook and flipped through a few pages until he came to the right one. "Monsieur Ledoux was killed between eleven P.M. and midnight. He was strangled with something made of leather and then he was thrown into the pool or fell into it."

I must have made some noise, because he abruptly stopped talking and rested his eyes on me instead. "I'm sorry to sound so cold. I see so much of this kind of thing. Maybe where you live, it's different. . . ."

"Sometimes," I said. "Was he already dead when he hit the water?" I heard the sound of my own voice, distant, as if coming out of an echo chamber.

He nodded and looked at me strangely. "Madame Ritchie, would it surprise you to know that your client took drugs before he died?"

My heart pounding inside my chest, I said, "What kind of drugs? How soon before he died?"

"We don't have all the test results, but probably a psychedelic. We'll know later. That's what it looks like right now."

I shook my head until I could feel my brains beginning to rattle around inside. "That's why I was protecting him, just like I told you yesterday. He wouldn't have taken anything on his own, I'm sure of it. He was still struggling with the effects from the last time. And he was so happy on Sunday night."

He wrote down something in his book. "What's your theory about the drug side of this, then? Did you suspect anyone after his last episode?"

I shook my head. "I didn't even know just what had happened for sure until we were here in Montreal."

"Mysterious son of a bitch," he said. "It got him killed. He should have talked to you."

I didn't have anything to add to that. "Do you have any suspects yet?"

He fixed his intense blue eyes on me and for a moment I wondered whether I was under suspicion myself. Almost as if he'd read my mind, he said, "Madame, I know all about the party on Sunday night and I have the names of everyone who was there. So don't worry—I know you didn't kill your client. And no, I don't know who did it. But I'm going to find out. *Garanti.*"

We talked a bit more, but my brain was buzzing so loudly I hardly heard what the man said. André had been drugged, strangled, and tossed into a swimming pool—dead—on the night of the greatest triumph of his life. There was no cop in the world scary enough to keep me out of this now. I would see to whoever had done this, if I had to see them in hell.

---

"You need some help," Raymond said. "And I've got just the person."

We were in his restaurant's kitchen. He was stirring a large pot of roux while I toyed with this idea and that. I knew that most murder cases are solved quickly or not at all, but my own feelings of loss and confusion were making me sluggish and dull-witted. Something had to give.

"What do you mean?" I asked. "I'm used to working alone."

"Yeah, but you don't have contacts here. And there's the language issue, too. Maybe not everyone would like to spill their guts to some American they've never seen before, and not everyone speaks good English. I know you're not that bad at French, but could you really conduct entire interviews without resorting to English?" He looked up from his stirring for a moment, his eyes filled with concern. "Think, Lil. You're not thinking."

He was right. For the last two days, I'd been going on automatic pilot, but that wouldn't be enough. I either had to act or give up, and I didn't believe in giving up. "So who's this person?"

Raymond smiled and nodded. "Good. His name is Serge Deschênes and you're gonna love him. He was born and raised in Montreal and knows every inch of this city, but he's not an earthling. He's from a planet far, far away and we're lucky he decided to visit with us."

I shook my head. "You're giving me an alien? I thought you said that's what I was."

"Different kind of alien," he said. "I call him the Zen Master behind his back, though as far as I know he never studied Eastern religion. He's just an incredibly savvy person and he'll help you cut through the bullshit. Trust me on this one, Lil."

"Okay," I said. "How soon can we meet? And for that matter, does he know anything about this?"

"Yeah, I called him a little while ago. Don't think I was trying to interfere with your business. I just wanted to check things out with Serge before I mentioned him to you. It turns out that he's been up to his neck in some project and would be glad for a distraction."

"How d' you know him?"

"We were lovers for about a month, years ago, when we were both still in our twenties. That was more or less a disaster at the time, but he's remained one of my best friends. We've seen each other at least once a week for years. I don't know what I'd do without him."

I hoped he wouldn't have to find out. "Okay," I said, "can you give him a call? We might as well check this out."

Serge was small and wiry, with an olive complexion and intelligent dark eyes that took in everything. A black beard flecked with bits of gray covered much of his face and he moved with a certain awareness of the physical that gave him a kind of grace. If I had seen him on the street as a stranger, his intensity might have caused me to guess terrorist or priest, but I would have guessed wrong.

He looked at me hard when we were introduced and I suddenly felt oddly exposed, but when he smiled, his face was transformed into that of a delighted child. "Lil Ritchie, I am very glad to meet with you. You are just what I need for a few days. An American woman!" he said, pronouncing *woman* as "woe-mun."

"And why is that?" I asked, not sure I wanted to know.

"Because I am sick of everyt'ing else. I see the same damn people every day, and here you are, so . . . so . . . different." He pronounced *different* the French way, "deef-er-aunt," and I smiled for the first time in two days.

Raymond sat us down out front with coffees and we talked over the events leading to André's death. Serge had heard of André and was livid that someone would kill an artiste, leaving the world with "cows and sheeps" instead. And, no offense to farm animals, I knew what he meant.

"I'm thinking it might be a good idea to go over to the hotel first and see if anyone will talk with us. The cops may have sworn the employees to secrecy, but there's often one or two who slip through the net."

"Sleep t'roo de net?"

"One or two who'll talk, anyway," I said. "Maybe someone who doesn't like cops."

"I myself hate cops. Except cute ones who like to dance."

I decided not to get into that for the time being. There was work to be done, and if this strangely reassuring man could help me, then we'd better get with on it before all the clues were washed, scrubbed, and sanitized away.

We headed off to the Hôtel Bienvenue with Raymond's good-bye kisses still fresh on our cheeks. I drove and Serge taught me the shortcuts.

---

The Hôtel Bienvenue sat high atop an office building on René Lévesque Boulevard, a street renamed in honor of the late premier who had put the Parti Québécois on the national and international political map. A fierce and eloquent defender of Québec's rights, he had helped usher in strong reforms that would, hopefully, assure French-speaking Québécois of a future in their small part of the huge behemoth called North America.

The hotel was well situated downtown, with a Métro stop just underneath. Its facade, while thoroughly modern, was elegant in a way many newer buildings seldom are; the architect obviously had had respect for the older buildings that gave the city its overall look, even adding to the impression of understated good taste they created. The lobby was large without being flashy, decorated in various shades of blues, from the velvet draperies to an engraved fleur-de-lis pattern running across the tops of the walls. It's the little things that tell, I thought, musing that in my country the fringe would probably be a row of eagles.

We peeked into the restaurants and bars just off the lobby before taking the elevator to the rooftop. When the doors opened, I was flooded with so many conflicting emotions that I had trouble making myself move. Without making a big deal about it, Serge patiently kept the doors from closing while I gathered myself together. Two nights ago, André had walked out of this very same elevator, a living man in triumph, and someone had seen to it that he wouldn't walk anywhere again. Sadness and anger are a powerful combination, and I felt at that moment like a loaded gun that could easily go off, hurting the innocent as well as the guilty.

I looked over at Serge, who leaned against the elevator doors, waiting. "You'll fix it, I t'ink," he said in his low growl.

"I'd better," I replied. "Because I'm of no use to anyone like this."

Without answering, he led me into the restaurant, whose glass walls overlooked the pool and garden and, beyond that, the jewel of Montreal herself. Waiters busily hustled to accommodate the lunch rush, so we bypassed them for the time being and headed outdoors. The sun beat down from a perfectly blue sky, but because of the building's height and proximity to the river, a stiff breeze kept things relatively cool. I stared off at the huge clock on top of the Molson's building in the distance, trying to delay looking directly at the pool and garden, getting my bearings.

When I finally turned around to face my surroundings, André's last moments took on a clarity I hadn't expected. There was the busy restaurant, even busier with summer tourists and festivalgoers; then the large rooftop garden, complete with trees and hedges and borders of flowers, designed to give hotel guests privacy and shade while they swam in the pool or enjoyed a cool drink while watching others in the sparkling water.

It would be all too easy to imagine some predator using the shadows from the trees as a perfect hiding place. I gazed into the water but could see nothing through my rage and sadness but a small, slight body hugging the bottom of the deep end.

When things slowed down in the restaurant, Serge and I spoke to a waiter he recognized, and, through this waiter, to others, but they all said the same thing. Since the festival had started, every night had been a zoo, and unless a customer behaved memorably, all the faces blended into one another and were easily replaced by the next order, the next drink, the next high or low tip.

We went back out to the pool area and discreetly nosed around for some small clue the cops had overlooked, something that would be the missing link leading to André's killer. But, of course, the hotel's housekeeping staff would have been instructed to restore the pool and garden area to its former orderliness and to do so quickly. We found nothing, not even a gum wrapper, for our trouble. Serge charmed the head of housekeeping into talking with us, but although she had every appearance of trying to be helpful, she remembered nothing useful.

We left the hotel and walked for a while along the busy downtown streets, Serge pointing out places of interest to me—a tobacco shop with a bookie in the back, a restaurant where a kingpin of the Montreal underworld held court. We went into a tiny bar and ordered cool draft beers, then sat there in relative silence, listening to the chatter around us.

Suddenly, Serge looked at me. "I just t'ought of somet'-ing," he said. "De city employs dese teenage boys to clean up after de concerts; my friend's boy do this every summer during the festival—makes good, good money. Mebbe one a dese kids see somet'ing. Nobody pay attention to dem, but dey see everyt'ing. I could ask."

I liked it.

I dropped Serge off on St-Laurent, where he needed to pick up some groceries, and we agreed to meet again in the early evening hours. We would talk to the boy together. I was too wiped out to do more without a nap, but not too tired to feel somewhat relieved. Raymond had been right—this man's help would be invaluable to me. I fell asleep sitting up in the overstuffed chair in my friend's living room, exhaustion finally laying me low.

# CHAPTER FIFTEEN

**A** f t e r
my nap, I visited with Ernie West. There were a couple of
things I'd been thinking of that needed to be attended to. Al
had gone to a movie, it turned out, so Ernie and I had a
chance to talk alone, something that hadn't really happened
since our day together in Tillman. The bass player was dressed
in old jeans and a sleeveless undershirt, and he didn't look as
if he had shaved since the day of the concert. When I arrived,
he was watching a French news channel, a beer in his hand.

"You understand that?" I asked, flopping down beside
him.

He shook his head. "Maybe I'll get it through osmosis or
something, but right now, I seem to understand only about
one word out of fifty." He turned off the sound on the set and
we sat there watching in silence for a few minutes.

"Ernie, I was wondering if you had talked with Irene at
all. I feel bad about not calling her up when all this happened, but I just couldn't seem to do it."

"I couldn't get ahold of her yesterday, so I called Lucie
instead. She said it would be better if she told her in person.
Later in the day, Irene called me here. She'd spoken with
Detective Rivard. She didn't sound so great."

"Will she come up here to claim the body?"

He sat there staring at the screen, then shook his head
again. "He's being shipped back home by a local funeral

146

parlor, tomorrow or the next day. I'd already identified him, so Irene didn't have to go through that, at least."

The experience didn't seem to have done Ernie any good, either. "How'd Lucie take it?"

"Bad," he said. "She worshiped André, ever since they were kids. But she's practical—she'll get through this somehow."

"I keep worrying about old Aunt Eulalie, in Brownville Junction. I assume Lucie called her, but I wonder if I should check in on her. She had a special thing going with André."

He nodded. "Yeah, she did. You know, he called her on Sunday, I think, in the morning. I was making coffee and heard him say her name, but then he took the phone into the bathroom, so I didn't really catch anything else."

"Really?" I thought about that for a bit. "Maybe he wanted her to catch the concert. Or maybe he was telling her about Lorraine."

"That was probably more like it," he said.

"Do you think he'd talked to Irene about Lorraine showing up yet?" I'd found myself wondering about that. Bringing a long-lost daughter into a troubled marriage would definitely be something to be negotiated carefully.

He shook his head. "Not as far as I know. Remember, André never was one to deal with things head-on. He probably wanted to sweet-talk Irene a little first, then bring it up. He was pretty good at that, when he wanted to be."

"Poor André," I said. "Life wasn't often kind to him."

"He wasn't kind to himself, either. But he didn't deserve to die like that."

Ernie's eyes filled up and he leaned back against the sofa and gazed toward the ceiling, wiping gruffly at the tears that ran down his cheeks. After a few minutes, he got up and came back with a fresh beer for himself and one for me. I didn't open mine up; I was tired and had more work to do.

"I might call up the aunt, see how she's doing," I said.

"Probably a good idea. It doesn't seem right that the old should lose someone younger, does it?"

It didn't, at that. "You staying here much longer?" I asked. The festival was over for these men.

"We're leaving tomorrow or the next day," he said, "like André."

Like André. I knew it was true, but I still found it hard to believe. I shook my head.

"Not everything's worked out, but I think there's gonna be a funeral service at the cathedral in Lewiston on Saturday afternoon. André would probably like it if you wanted to come." He said this with his eyes fixed firmly on the screen, in the flattened tones of sorrow.

I said I'd be there. After we'd said good-bye, I stood there in the hallway, listening again to the sounds of the news being reported in French. There had been a fire in Dorval, a possible arson. There was talk of a probable Métro strike by the maintenance workers. Some rain was to be expected in the next day or two.

I closed my eyes and searched for the strains of music I'd heard from the same loft only a couple of days ago. I could remember, but memory wasn't even remotely the same as hearing.

---

While Raymond went to Chinatown to pick up our takeout from the Sun-Sun Café, I steeled myself to make the call to Aunt Eulalie. If I always had the instinct to protect the old from other people's deaths, I also reminded myself that the elderly have had a lot more practice in dealing with it than the young. I might as well get it over with.

The phone rang for a long time and I was about to hang up when I realized someone had finally answered. "Hello," I said. "Mrs. Tremblay, this is Lil Ritchie. I thought I'd see how you're feeling."

There was silence on the other end of the line for a

second or two and then a hesitant male voice said, "This is not the lady of the house. This is a neighbor of hers, come to help out."

Help out? I thought. Had the old lady collapsed? "I see," I said. "Do you know when I might speak with Mrs. Tremblay?"

The man again hesitated, and I could hear a woman's voice asking him to find out who was calling. Then the man, sounding embarrassed, said, "Just a minute, my wife . . ." and a woman's voice came over the wire.

"Hello?" she said. "Who is this?"

What was going on? "I'm an acquaintance of Mrs. Tremblay's and I was calling to see if she was all right." I told her my name.

"All right?" she said. "All right? No, Mrs. Tremblay is not all right. She's in the hospital right now, fighting for her life."

The woman's voice trembled, and this time I could hear her husband nervously consoling her.

I stood up. Oh God, I thought. I knew the news would be too much for her. "Did she have a stroke or something?" I asked. "What hospital is she in?"

"Excuse me, I can't talk," the woman mumbled, then the man's voice came back on the line. "Ma'am, we're sorry about telling you like this, but we're upset as all get-out. We're the Loudens, from up the road. Mrs. Tremblay was attacked here in the wee morning hours. She's hurt pretty bad and they're not sure she's gonna make it. The sheriff said we could come over and get some things for her—her robe and whatnot."

I sat back down, all the starch knocked out of me. Attacked? In Brownville Junction? Nothing made sense. "Do you know what happened yet?" I asked. "Who would do this to an old lady?"

"Well, they figure she either let 'em in herself or she didn't have the door latched. I s'pose either one's possible— we all know each other around here and she wasn't much one for lockin' up. Anyway, they 'bout beat the poor old thing near to death."

My heart was pounding so hard, I could feel it through my clothes. "What hospital did they take her to, Mr. Louden?"

"Down to Bangor. They got the most modern equipment around here."

I thanked him, I think, before hanging up the phone. I called Serge, who said he would speak with his friend's son himself in my absence. It was a long shot, but it would be worth a try. I made another few calls—to Lorraine, to whom I did not give the latest news, and to Ernie West, who was not so lucky. Molly would meet me at the hospital in six hours in case I needed a lawyer in order to be let into the old woman's room.

By the time Raymond returned home with the food, my bags were packed and stashed inside the car. I wasn't the least bit hungry, but he threw me the container of egg rolls, anyway. I gassed up the car and checked the oil at a station on Papineau, near the Jacques Cartier Bridge, then raced a cabbie through a red light. It was a seven-hour trip, but I intended to do it in six hours, or maybe even five if the Subaru held up.

I crossed the bridge in the fast lane, glancing once into the rearview mirror to watch the lights of Montreal recede into the distance.

---

Traffic on the autoroute was light, and I took full advantage, pushing the old car relentlessly—to seventy, seventy-five, then eighty. At eighty, the car started shaking like a dog who's just swum in the creek, so I slowed the needle down to a steady seventy-five and kept it there. The Townships passed by me in a blur, this time capturing neither my thoughts nor my attention.

When I stopped at the border, I noticed that the Subaru

150

smelled hot, so I had the attendant at the gas station on the U.S. side check the oil again. When he opened up the hood, we could see the heat radiating off the motor like a shimmer in the desert. "Whooee," he said. "This horse has sure been rid! You better let her cool off some."

"Later," I said. "I've got a date."

He looked at me strangely, then added some oil and filled the tank with some expensive border gas. I bought a couple of coffees to go and a pack of Camels, then sped off down the road. Just past the Chain of Ponds, a pair of moose stood idly in the road, so I braked hard, coming to a stop just a few feet away from several tons of hoof and antler. I sat there sideways in the road, my breath coming in gasps, while the two scrambled awkwardly up a steep bank and into the woods.

By the time I reached Newport, I was crazy with road fatigue, so I stopped a few minutes for something to eat. It wouldn't take me long to reach Bangor now and I needed to be coherent in case they let me talk to Aunt Eulalie. Glancing at my face in the bathroom mirror, I saw a bleary-eyed maniac staring back. I splashed myself with cold water and ran a comb through my hair; it would have to do.

Halfway between Newport and Bangor, the awful pictures that I had managed to keep at bay during this long, punishing drive now came unbidden into my mind. I saw André struggling as someone squeezed the life-breath out of him. I saw him hit the water and slowly sink to the bottom. I saw Aunt Eulalie mauled by an assailant in her little house by the road. Shuddering, I attempted to substitute happier pictures—André playing his guitar on his aunt's porch; the old woman taking *tourtière* out of the oven. But these images were no less painful to me.

At Bangor, I drove straight to the hospital and pulled into a parking space in the lot. I turned off the motor and sat there for a few minutes, listening to the little clicking noises the car made as the motor cooled. I glanced at my watch—I had made it from Montreal to Bangor in five and a half hours.

Inside, I spoke with the receptionist at the main desk, who confirmed that a Eulalie Tremblay had been admitted to the hospital's intensive-care unit. I walked past the elevators, down a long hallway, and found myself facing a brightly lit room. I glanced at the nurses' station, where two nurses appeared to be conferring over a patient's chart; when they didn't turn around, I ducked into the room. The patients were separated into their own little cubicles, with a glass in front so the nurses could keep an eye out. The place had an eerie sound, I thought, then realized it was from various machines that hissed and hummed life into the patients who lay there motionless.

I walked past the first bed—no, that was a young man; then the second, a very pregnant woman, with tubes and wires everywhere. With my skin prickling uncomfortably and sour sweat streaming from my armpits, I made it to the third cubicle. There, a large, gray-haired old woman lay, her belly making a mound in the sheets like a gentle hill. I stopped in my tracks, taking in the machines that tracked her every breath and the waxy pallor of her skin. The old lady's face was one large bruise, an angry purple and blue, and what I could see of her body was not much different.

It was Aunt Eulalie.

"Oh no," I said out loud. "Oh God, no." Then a nurse came running full tilt, followed by another. The first one tried putting an arm around me in a comforting gesture, but I shook it off angrily.

"Get your hands off me," I said in a voice I barely recognized. "Just keep your hands to yourself."

The nurses stepped back, throwing each other a quick glance. Did they have a crazy on their hands?

I took a deep breath, then another, and turned and walked back out to the hallway without another word, the nurses following closely behind, like sheepdogs rounding up a stray. Shaking all over, I sank into an orange plastic chair and accepted the little paper cone of water that was handed to me. But the lump of rage was caught in my throat and I found I couldn't swallow.

I was still holding the water when Molly walked into the room and gently removed it from my hand. She said something quietly to the nurses and they nodded in response, but I never heard what it was. We walked out of there together and kept on walking until the urge to kill had left me. Then we walked some more just to make sure.

---

"They're not going to let you anywhere near her," Molly said. "You're not a relative, and the night nurses don't like you much." Molly was sitting on the edge of the bed I was occupying in the Riverfront Motel, a couple of blocks from the hospital. We had both decided I was too tired and strung out to do anything more until I'd at least stretched out quietly for a few hours.

"I didn't say that much to them."

"Uh-huh," she said. "It's not so much what you actually said, Lil, as the Charlie Manson vibes you were giving off." She looked at me for a few minutes, while I more or less concentrated on the water marks on the ceiling.

"You want me to stay?" she said after a while. "I've got court in the morning, but I could get there from here just as well."

I propped myself up on an elbow. "Nah, you better get home and get ready for your case. I'll be all right if I can just get a little sleep."

She nodded. "Okay. But give me a call tomorrow when you know what's what, would you?"

I said that I would.

She slipped on her sandals and stood up. "You think the two things are related? Someone wanted them both dead?"

"Well, it's a pretty big coincidence otherwise." My head hurt like hell and I'd bottomed out on whatever reserves of energy I'd been running on.

I stood up to walk Molly to the door. "Thanks, old pal," I said, hugging her. "I'm lucky you know me so well, especially tonight."

"Goes both ways, Lil. Now call me when you know something, so I don't worry, okay?"

I watched her drive off, locked the door, and fell tiredly upon the bed and into a deep sleep.

---

In the morning, I made a few phone calls, one of them to an orderly I knew. I treated myself to a breakfast of lox and eggs at the Bagel Shop, accompanied by an egg bagel fresh out of the oven. As I munched, I compared the taste and texture of Bangor and Montreal bagels and resolved to get an authoritative history of the different schools of bagel making sometime soon. These were the thoughts of a person running on empty in more ways than one. I'd been doing it for a while, and last night it had caught up with me. I wouldn't make that mistake twice.

This time when I entered the hospital, I veered away from the receptionist area and took the elevator down a flight. A sleepy-looking man wearing a tool belt and carrying a spool of wire waited to get on. I smiled at him and he nodded. "This place starts up too damn early in the day for me. Went off without my lab coat this time."

"They been drying and folding over there," he said. "Grab you another one. They're used to it."

I followed the sounds of washing machines and dryers and came upon four women folding, as the man had said, and yakking and smoking, as well. A coffeepot sat almost empty on a metal stand. The women looked up as I entered the room.

"Forgot my lab coat," I said, smiling apologetically. "Got anything that'd fit me?"

The oldest woman frowned at me. "Don't remember seein' ya down here before," she said. "Ya new?"

"Don't I look it?"

Her companions laughed at this, and the woman, sighing, pointed to a nearby rack. "Over there, but don't mess up the others—we just finished hanging that bunch."

The floor the women stood on was cement, which made the room seem damp, in spite of the heat from the dryers. I tried on a jacket. "They pay you right?" I asked. "Working in a laundry's hard work."

The women looked at one another and laughed. "This work ain't so hard," one of them said. "Stayin' at home with my old man's what's hard."

Their laughter accompanied me back to the elevator, where I buttoned up the coat and said my little liar's prayer. Once inside, I pushed the first-floor button and took a couple of deep breaths. Clutching the clipboard I'd purchased earlier at Newberry's to my chest, I exited the elevator and walked determinedly back to ICU, nodding hello to the nurses as I passed. Thank God for the day shift, I thought.

Steeling myself as I entered the patient area, I noticed the pregnant woman had her eyes open this time. A nurse, or aide, was busy taking her vital signs. Although my heart sped up for a few beats, she paid me no attention. This is too easy, I thought.

When I reached Eulalie's cubicle, I did a double take; the bed was empty. I whirled around, looking wildly for the old woman, and this time the nurse looked up. "They moved her up to the fifth floor," she said quietly. "Head injuries."

"You'd think they'd tell us, too," I said with a trace of irritation in my voice. "Oh well. Catch ya later."

I got back into the elevator, sweating now. I wondered

what this meant. Was the old woman better and was that why they had moved her? Or was she worse?

I again exited the elevator, looking around this time. This was a normal hospital floor and I saw everywhere the flurry of movement that characterize the work of a day shift. Patients were being washed and dressed; bandages were being changed; doctors were making their rounds. Near the elevator, I read a sign with arrows in both directions: Neurology was to the left and Ear, Nose, and Throat to the right. I followed the arrow to the left.

At the nurse's station, I paused and wrote down something on my clipboard. The ward clerk looked up. "Mrs. Tremblay's room number, please?" I smiled. "They forgot to tell me they'd moved her."

"So what else is new?" she said, turning to sign something a doctor placed before her. "She's in room five thirty-eight, but don't expect too much. She's pretty out of it."

"That's okay," I said. "Just need to glance in for a sec."

Although it was a double room, the old woman was alone in it, her eyes still closed, her breathing regular but slow. She had tubes in her arms, which were strapped down and looked uncomfortably tight. She was still wearing a colorless hospital gown, so either the doctors hadn't allowed the Loudens in with her own things or she was in such bad shape that she didn't need them. Again, looking at her was painful, but I forced myself to take some more deep breaths and remember why I was there. A repeat performance of my visit last night would only cost me valuable time.

I walked over and closed the door, then dragged a visitor's chair over to the side of the bed. I took Aunt Eulalie's left hand in mine and stroked it lightly, feeling the rough calluses she'd formed in a lifetime of washing and scrubbing and weeding. This wasn't my beloved old aunt—she'd belonged to André—but I loved her some just the same for being who she was.

After a few minutes, I stood up and rubbed her forehead as lightly as I could, feeling the heat in the bruising there and seeing up close the puffiness under her eyelids. "I'm so sorry," I said to her quietly. "I'm so very, very sorry this happened to you. You didn't deserve this."

After a few minutes, she stirred slightly and moved her head a little from one side to the other. I kept on stroking her, feeling less than useless, suddenly wondering what I'd hoped to accomplish in this room. The old woman needed medical help, not hand-holding, not my probing.

I was thinking dark thoughts when she opened her eyes wide and looked directly at me. She groaned and I stepped back, wondering whether I should be so bold as to summon a nurse. No, I thought, I'll just be quick and notify them on my way out that she's awake.

"Hello, Tante Eulalie," I said in André's form of address as I took her hand again. She said nothing, but I felt her squeeze my own hand slightly. I leaned down toward her, talking softly. "I'm so sorry this happened to you, Tante Eulalie. You're safe now, so just keep resting. Everything will be all right."

She whispered something. I couldn't hear what she said, so I leaned in still closer. "What did you say? Tell me again if you can."

*"Y'ont tué mon beau gars,"* she whispered.

For a moment, I panicked at the sounds of country French coming from her lips, but then I made myself repeat the sentence slowly in my mind, one word at a time. My eyes teared up when I realized what the old woman had said: "They killed my beautiful boy."

They certainly had. And someone had nearly succeeded in killing her, as well. "I'll find out who did that, Mrs. Tremblay. I'll promise you that." I squeezed her hand. "Mrs. Tremblay, do you know who did this to you?"

She closed her eyes again and for a moment I thought

157

she was asleep. *"J'le connais pas, mais je l'ai vu à la TV,"* she said, and again she fixed me with her fierce gaze. *"Y'est à la TV."*

He's on the television? What the hell did that mean?

"Who do you mean?" I asked. "Who's on the TV?" She seemed to be following her thoughts and reliving a terrible experience.

*"C't un démon!"* she said, the intensity of her feeling filling the room. *"C't un démon!"* She now moved her head rapidly from side to side, agitated, and I feared she would hurt herself.

"I know, I know," I soothed, rubbing her silver hair gently. "Shhh . . . just rest now, Mrs. Tremblay. You need to get your strength back. Try not to think about these bad things. You're safe here and in good hands."

After a few minutes, she did fall back to sleep without saying anything more. I stroked her for a few moments longer, then moved the visitor's chair back to its spot against the radiator. "I'll find him for you, I swear," I whispered, and I kissed her on the forehead before leaving the room.

I walked back toward the nurses's station. The ward clerk looked up. "Mrs. Tremblay's been in and out," I said. "Might check on her, see if she needs any medication."

The busy clerk nodded. "Thanks. Dr. Baker's on his way up to see her. I'll tell him."

I took the elevator back down, stopping at the florist's downstairs to send up a pot of African violets to room 538.

I started up the Subaru, then turned off the motor when I realized I didn't know where I was going next. André's aunt had tried to tell me something, but what had it meant? Who was on the TV? Who was a demon? Had she given me a lead, or were these just the ravings of a distressed old woman with a head injury?

Then I remembered the morning I had left her house with André in tow. The old woman had tried to tell me something then, too, but I hadn't had enough information to process it. She had told me to take care of her nephew and I had promised her I would. And now someone *had* killed her beautiful boy. She had known all along what was going on.

Now I remembered Ernie West saying only yesterday that André had called his aunt on Sunday morning, just hours before he was killed. He had told her something new and maybe that's what had gotten them both into trouble.

Who was the demon on the TV?

# CHAPTER SIXTEEN

G u i l t y
over the shameful way I'd treated the Subaru the day before,
I spent a little time having her oil changed at Midas Muffler.
They checked her fluids as well and all the belts. The old car
had stood by me when I hadn't deserved it, so I patted her
special spot on the dash lovingly and sweet-talked her all the
way out of Bangor.

It was raining lightly when I turned off the interstate
toward Brownville Junction. I rolled the windows up and took
my time, the windshield wipers' drone reminding me that I
hadn't had a lot of sleep in the last few days. I turned on the
radio and listened to a country station for a little while, then
turned it off, dissatisfied. This was no time for the young
cowboy-hatted, hip-grinding boys the disc jockey was playing—this sad day should belong to Hank Williams or George
Jones or Patsy Cline.

At Milo, I began to have serious doubts about my plans.
The cops had already been all over the old woman's house.
What did I hope to find that they'd missed? But I still felt I
might have an advantage over the sheriff's boys. They were
coming in cold, after all. I had recently spent a long afternoon alone in the house, so I might notice a change in the
decor. By the time I reached Brownville, I had convinced
myself I was doing the right thing.

At the Junction I slowed down, not wanting to call undue attention to myself. When I passed the little frame house, I looked for other cars, but Aunt Eulalie's Buick was the only car there. I drove on for another mile, noticing the Loudens' place—without their car. I then turned around and parked in a pull-off spot near a creek, in sight of the Tremblay home. Closing the car door quietly, I ducked into the woods.

On another day, I would probably have enjoyed my hike through the forest. The little creek hummed with life, mosses and ferns grew abundantly around its banks, and both blue-and-white periwinkles, or myrtle, gave the rich bottomland a cheerful ground cover. But I could have used a machete to crash through the undergrowth that kept tripping me up. Praying that none of it was poison oak, which I had forgotten how to identify, I worked my way up and around the hill, huffing and puffing a bit in the damp air. The cigarette smoking would have to go, I thought. But a few minutes later, I'd reached my destination, a little stand of silver birches marking the edge of the Tremblay property. So far, so good.

I jogged across the backyard and peered into the house through the kitchen window. I checked the windows I could reach, listening for even faint sounds within. Nothing. Then I used my library card to jimmy the lock on the back door and entered the house. I stood in the kitchen for a minute or two, still listening, until the cuckoo clock struck the half-hour and I nearly jumped out of my skin, as spooked as a horse who's smelled a bear. "Get a grip!" I said, my voice sounding loud in the emptiness surrounding me.

I went through the house methodically, room by room, touching nothing but looking everywhere for anything that didn't seem right. Aunt Eulalie had obviously been attacked in the front part of the house, and from the looks of the sitting room, she'd put up quite a fight. A chest of drawers had been dragged away from a wall and one of the overstuffed chairs was still lying on its side. It was on the floor at the edge of the hallway that she'd lost the battle, dark stains marking the spot where she'd lain and bled.

It occurred to me that I'd never found out how she'd gotten help. I'd try asking her, for starters, then the Loudens, if it came to that. Leaning on the doorjamb, looking at the mess in the sitting room, I knew Aunt Eulalie would hate the way her home had been left, she who had probably never once gone to bed with dishes in the sink or left a floor unscrubbed that needed scrubbing. Things would have to be straightened up before she came home.

Moving on, I made a closer inspection of the sitting room, even getting down on all fours to see under the furniture. Just when I'd decided I was wasting my time, I noticed something sticking out from behind the knocked-over chair—a matchbook. I picked it up and turned it over in my hand, not quite believing what my eyes were telling me: The matchbook was black and shiny, with elegant gold lettering that advertised Le Sieur de Champlain, one of the rooftop restaurants at the Hôtel Bienvenue in Montreal. "Holy shit," I muttered. Hardly daring to breathe, I opened it up. Inside, someone had scrawled a phone number with a light pencil, in a sloping hand.

The matchbook all but burned my fingers. Although it fell short of giving the name and address of André's murderer, it linked him with the attack on Aunt Eulalie. Someone had killed André late on Sunday and then attempted to do the same to his aunt the following night. But he'd made one mistake.

I closed the house back up and all but skipped through the woods. If I hurried, I could be back in Bangor by visiting hours. If Aunt Eulalie was better, I would show her what I had found and her eyes would tell me what it meant.

———

By the time I neared Bangor, the sun was coming out, which I took as a good sign. I'd finally seen a tiny light at the end of the dark tunnel I'd been laboring in ever since I'd started my investigation. Information had been flitting around me all along like the hum of mosquitoes, but I hadn't been able to make sense of it. Now I could feel a subtle shift.

I spent several minutes looking for a parking space in the hospital lot, finally squeezing in between a camper and a pickup. I had to suck in my gut to get out. Some people can't park any better than they drive. I stopped at the gift shop and bought Aunt Eulalie a small box of chocolates for when she was feeling better; I also picked up a copy of *Down East* magazine, as well. Even if she wasn't in any shape to read for a while, the photographs might cheer her up.

Coming out of the gift shop, I heard a commotion and turned toward the sound. Lucie Pinkham was tearing out of the elevator, followed by the priest I'd met in Lewiston—what was his name?

"Lucie!" he called. "Wait!" I looked about in momentary confusion as she ran toward me, apparently headed for the front entrance. She was crying. The priest spotted me standing there. "Stop her," he called out.

I stepped in front of her a little too late and she crunched down on my sneakered foot before she was able to stop. Dropping the magazine and the chocolates, I touched her on the arm. "Lucie," I said, "It's me, Lil Ritchie. What's wrong?" The priest made it to her side and I quickly reached down to gather up my belongings before someone tripped over them.

"Please!" Lucie wailed to the priest. "Just let me go outside, Father. If I don't get some air, I'm going to suffocate." I looked at her in alarm. Lucie Pinkham had struck me as a person with a strong sense of herself and of her strengths. But the woman I saw before me was breathing shallowly, in little gasps, her color unhealthily pale. Had she freaked out when she'd seen what they'd done to Eulalie, as I had the previous night, or had something even worse happened?

I took her by the arm, flashing the priest a look. "C'mon, Lucie, let's get that air. I don't think much of hospitals, either." With a good dozen people staring, we made it out the front entrance and stood there in silence for a few minutes while Lucie got some air in her lungs. After a bit, she began breathing more normally and looked around at her surroundings for the first time. "Do you think we could sit down?" she said. "I'm not feelin' so good." An elderly man heard her and slowly rose from the bench he was occupying. "Have yourself a seat right here," he said. "I was just about to get up, anyway."

Lucie and the priest—Father Jean-Pierre, I finally remembered—sat down on the bench and he took her hand and patted it. I stood there awkwardly, not sure I wanted to hear the answer to the question I needed to ask. Then Lucie looked directly at me for the first time. "You know my brother is dead," she said.

I nodded. "I'm as sorry as I can be, Lucie."

She sniffled and rummaged through her purse for a tissue. "And now my aunt, too!" she said, starting to cry again in earnest.

The feelings of denial I had been nurturing for the last five minutes or so abandoned me abruptly. Just this morning, I had talked with the old woman and held her hand, and now she was gone.

The priest cleared his throat. "Madame Tremblay passed away an hour ago, poor soul. We were there with her when it happened—cardiac arrest. The staff tried to resuscitate her, but there was nothing they could do."

My knees suddenly turned to rubber, I slid onto the bench next to Lucie. Aunt Eulalie was dead? The old feeling of rage came rising back up, but for Lucie's sake, I sat there quietly until I gained a modicum of control. She had all she could handle as it was—first her brother, then her aunt.

I sighed and the three of us sat there in silence for a few minutes. A breeze rustled the leaves on the little maple next to us and a steady stream of cars stopped and started at the set of lights just beyond the lot. Someone honked a horn. A truck headed up the hill, dragging its muffler, making little metallic *bings* with each bump. We heard snippets of low conversation as relatives and friends walked in and out of the hospital carrying flowers or candy.

Finally, I spoke and time moved again. "She was a great old woman, Lucie. I feel privileged to have known her at all." I meant it.

"Thanks," she said. "I didn't see her as often as I should've, but I loved her and she knew it." Lucie tugged at the Kleenex in her hand. Suddenly, she looked at me. "Are you looking for whoever killed my brother?"

Surprised at her directness, I nodded. "I won't stop until I find who did it, either."

Father Jean-Pierre shifted his position on the bench. "It was a sad, sad thing to have happened," he said. "When we met, you were looking for him. Did you ever find him?"

"Not really," I answered. "Although I did spend a lot of time with him."

The priest looked at me oddly, then let the matter drop. Now it was my turn. "I think the person who murdered André is the same person who assaulted Mrs. Tremblay. I wouldn't bring it up at a time like this, except . . . well, I don't feel I have a choice. Whoever did this is now responsible for two deaths, and they have to be stopped."

"Won't the police find this person?" The priest was used to working with large organizations.

"They might," I said. "But I'm already involved. If they

solve this first, then okay, it's done. But meanwhile, I've got some work to do."

"Good," Lucie said, the power in her voice surprising me. I looked at her. "I've got to finish this," I said.

"Yes, you do. I'll pay you whatever you charge, when this is over. I just need to know, you understand?" Her eyes implored me to follow her meaning. "Someone should be made to pay."

The priest muttered something under his breath. When we turned toward him, he repeated what he'd said: "Justice is mine, sayeth the Lord."

It's everybody's, I thought, but I didn't say it.

"Lucie, I've been wondering about something. Did André ever even talk to you on the telephone, saying he was going to return the money? Or did he fake that whole conversation from your aunt's house, with me standing right there?"

She lowered her head a little, embarrassed, I thought.

"No, the call was real."

"Then did you know he wasn't going to show up at your house, or did he leave you hanging again?"

She glanced at the priest.

"Remember when he said to get in touch with Uncle Roland? Well, that's a signal we've used since we were kids, meaning 'this is all made up and I'll explain later.' Uncle Roland died in 1950."

Damn, I thought, the guy was good.

After a while, it was time for them to go and I walked them back to Lucie's car. "How's Irene holding up?" I asked. "I've got to call her, but things have been a little crazy."

Lucie laughed bitterly. "I'll never understand that woman," she said. "I know she's upset, but she's being a regular pain in the neck, insisting on a Baptist funeral when André's been a Catholic all his life."

I hadn't thought about that. Father Jean-Pierre spoke

166

up. "I'm sure she doesn't realize how important a good Catholic funeral is to someone of the faith. I've elected to be the one to talk with her about this when we get back home. It's a sensitive issue for all involved, but I feel we can work it out."

"When's the funeral?" I asked. "Ernie said something about Saturday."

"Well, we have to clear this up with Irene first, but . . . I don't know what you think about this, Father, but could André and Aunt Eulalie have a double funeral Mass?"

He widened his eyes, considering Lucie's question. "Such tragedy," he said finally, shaking his head. "Let me see what I can do with your brother's wife first, Lucie, and then we can talk about a double funeral. And then there's Eulalie's own priest to consider. We'll have to work this out, but yes, I believe it would be possible."

That's what death is like, I thought, as I watched them drive away. One minute you're eating *tourtière* with someone or playing music, and the next thing you know, poof . . . they're gone, like a bubble that's burst.

I walked back into the hospital to use the pay phone to call Molly. Noticing a poor-looking family with a bunch of little kids standing by the elevators, I handed the littlest one the box of chocolates and the magazine. "Think you can use this?" I asked. His eyes lit up. "I'll take them to my grammy," he said proudly, reaching out with both hands to take the packages carefully from me.

His mother spoke up. "You sure you can't use 'em yourself?" she asked.

I shook my head and the woman seemed to understand.

"You tell your grammy to get better soon," I said, and the boy nodded somberly.

Then I walked over to the phone booth, my feet as heavy as lead.

"Thank goodness you called," Molly said. "This Serge has called three times and I didn't have any way to get in touch with you."

What now? The world was starting to spin a little too fast, I thought. "Aunt Eulalie died a little while ago," I told Molly. "Her heart gave out."

"Shit," she said softly, then added, "I'm sorry, Lil."

I didn't say anything for a minute.

"You still there?"

"Yeah," I said gruffly. "Sorry. And you know what? Whoever beat her up just went straight from assault and battery to murder one."

"He did indeed. But, Lil, you know this also means that the Attorney General's boys will be working on the case now. Those Augusta guys get up there, they won't take kindly to a private detective doing it her way."

"I know. But there have been times when they've exchanged information or worked loosely with private cops. Remember the one Bart was talking about? The woman who was shot by those deputies?"

Bart was a cop friend of Molly's. "That's true," she admitted, "but that private cop would have to work on a team, and we all know how hard that is for some people."

She had a point, but I didn't feel like getting into that right now, so I changed the subject. "What did Serge say?"

"Well, the first two times, he didn't leave a message. The last time, he said to tell you that he had talked with a couple of boys and had found out something very interesting. He wants you to call him back."

"Okay. Maybe I'll try to get him now. You be there for a while?"

"Yeah."

We hung up and I dug around in my wallet for a few minutes, looking for my long-distance calling card, which finally showed up underneath a fifth-grade picture of my sister. Serge answered on the first ring, not bothering to hide the excitement in his voice. "I 'ave some news for you, Lil. It's good, good, good."

When he told me what he'd found out, I had to agree with him. We made plans to meet the next day—I'd call him when I arrived—and then I hung up and checked in with Raymond.

Molly must've been sitting on the phone. "Guess what," I told her, and then I filled her in on what Serge had uncovered.

She whistled low. "You've got to get back up there," she said. "But why drive it? You're exhausted, Lil. Don't forget, there's this train at Brownville Junction that leaves at something like midnight. You could sleep on the way."

That was an idea. Canadian Pacific Railways ran a train, the Atlantic, a branch of its national VIA system, that started at Saint John, New Brunswick, and crossed the top of the State of Maine, entering at Mattawamkeag. It stopped at Brownville Junction and Greenville before crossing the international border to Mégantic, Sherbrooke, and points west, berthing in Montreal just in time for breakfast. There was talk of the Canadian government's plans to discontinue the passenger line, which it had already cut down from daily runs to three trips a week, but for now the CP train was still the only direct link to Québec other than driving.

The train's schedule enabled me to go home for a few hours and see whether my cat was still speaking to me, make some important calls, and pick up a change of wardrobe. Then I could drive back to Brownville Junction for the second time that day and leave my car at the station. I'd have seven hours of being rocked to sleep by the train, something that always worked well for me.

"Okay," I said. "You've made a convincing case—for a lawyer. I'll leave here now and see if my house is still standing."

"Want some supper together?"

"If I can eat, yeah."

I left Bangor before the five o'clock rush and made it to Tillman in a flash. Then I sat on my little back stoop and watched Littlefield stalk crickets for a while, drinking a Corona while I thought about what was coming.

Each and every investigation is different, but to me, they're all a circle. You start out not knowing much and there's this tiny circle, and then, as more facts are uncovered, the circle expands just a little. The more you know, the more there is to know. Then at a certain point, the circle rapidly grows and grows with each new shred of information, until it suddenly can't contain itself anymore. Then it's as if the circle opens up, almost of its own volition. And that's when a good detective jumps in. At that point, no amount of maneuvering by the guilty parties can ever close it back up again. It's too late.

---

By nine-thirty, I was sitting behind the steering wheel once again, with Molly and Littlefield looking on. Molly was rare in Littlefield's book—he not only suffered being held by her but usually purred while she was doing it. Chemistry, I guess. "You two make quite the little couple," I said. "Won't your attorney friend get jealous?" Molly sighed. "I doubt it. That would be a human emotion, and he's not too good with those."

"Hmmm. Well, you doing okay? Holding your own?"

"Yeah, Lil. Don't worry. You've got enough to think about already, seems to me. You get back home and we'll catch up on my pitiful emotional life."

"You got a date," I said. I backed out of the driveway, remembered something, and drove back in. "If I need a phone number traced, you think Bart could get it done?"

"If I twist his arm a little."

I wrote down the number I'd found on the matchbook

and handed it to Molly. "It might not be anything important, or then again, it could be. It might even be Canadian."

She looked at it. "He's got these buddies all over the state—from the Police Academy. You call on any law-enforcement outfit in Maine, chances are Bart went to school with at least one person there. Anyway, I happen to know that he has computer guys among his friends. I'll get this to him first thing tomorrow."

"You're too good to me," I said, backing out again.

"I know it," she called. "Get some sleep."

Sleep was definitely on my mind the nearer I got to my destination. Small towns often close down early, and as I drove past the dark houses of Milo and Brownville, I began to feel as if I were the last person awake in the world. But the train station was well-lit, and felt cheery. The parking lot was starting to fill up for the Atlantic's quick midnight stop. I locked up the Subaru and gave her a good-bye pat. "Be here when I get back at the ungodly hour of three-thirty in the morning," I said. That was the only unfortunate thing about taking this train—you had to catch it at midnight, and on the return trip you were stranded, confused, and half-asleep in the middle of nowhere three hours before sunrise. Otherwise, it was a perfect means of transportation.

Inside, the place was hopping with passengers and crew. I recognized a friendly conductor busy making a fresh pot of coffee. When it finished brewing, I bought a cup and took it outside, walking up and down the platform alongside parked freight cars, sipping and thinking. I was still trying to digest the fact that André, someone I'd known, liked, and respected, had been murdered, when Eulalie's violent death had compounded the case. Who would ever want to kill that wonderful, completely harmless old woman? What danger could she have represented and to whom? My head ached.

Passengers began to gather on the platform and bags were wheeled out. A steady, bright cyclops light slowly approached. The train was arriving. Good-byes were hastily exchanged, people grouped in three or four different spots to board. As the train inched along, I saw seemingly empty, darkened cars. From past experience, I knew these coaches were filled with people sleeping in every possible uncomfortable position, sprawled across two seats when possible, or with little pillows jammed against the windows. In my state of exhaustion, I felt a stab of envy and longed for a corner for my bones.

Soon I was ushered into a separate three-car section filled with those who had embarked in the United States and would have to clear customs. Sinking into a seat behind a young mother and child, in which no one joined me, I took off my shoes and curled up. Soon I was traveling through the dark, deep Maine wilderness where white and silver birches occasionally lit up the landscape as we passed. After a while, the head conductor came by, a black man from Nova Scotia named Johnson, famous among train riders for his habit of memorizing the name and seat number of each passenger.

"Miss Ritchie!" he exclaimed. "It's been a long while since I've seen you! Is it a pleasure trip or business this time?"

"Business, Mr. Johnson, but I'm so tired that this part is pleasure in the extreme."

He nodded and smiled. "We'll turn the lights off in a minute or two, then you can rest. Other than the border people, I don't expect you'll be kept awake on my train," he said proudly.

He was right. I balled up the tiny little pillow they furnished, wrapped a blanket around me, and took my place among the sleepers leaning against the windows. I woke up once, groggily, and handed the customs men my filled out information card. No, I wasn't carrying liquor or tobacco or plants or, for that matter, a firearm. I fell back to sleep immediately, not waking this time until the light began to seep in around Sherbrooke, Québec. After that, I snoozed intermittently until we approached Montreal. As the train crossed Victoria Bridge, I stood and stretched, rubbing my sore neck until the blood seemed to flow in it again. Drinking indifferent CP coffee, I admired the downtown skyline etched against the mound of Mount Royal. The city was beautiful in the soft early-morning light and it was hard to imagine that there was violence or hurt or hunger within its borders.

Canadian gun laws are strict and the likelihood of dying a violent death in Canada is small, but still, every now and then it happens. By coming to Montreal, had André enticed his killer to follow him, drawing a murderer from Maine or parts unknown, or had there been a Canadian connection all along that I had known nothing about?

■ ■ ■ ■ ■ ■ ■ ■ ■ ■ ■ ■ ■ ■ ■ ■ ■ ■ ■ ■

# CHAPTER SEVENTEEN

I took a cab over to Raymond's, stopping once to grab a bag of breakfast empanadas from a Chilean joint near The Main. Their smell filled the cab and my stomach started rumbling. "Ya hungry?" The driver smiled at me through the rearview. "Me, I never eat 'til noon."

"If I waited until then, I'd eat your whole cab," I said, and he chuckled. The cabbie was a man in his sixties or so, with kind eyes and a head full of wavy gray hair. The dashboard, I noticed, was decorated with pictures of the Virgin Mary.

Raymond met me at the door, coffee mug in hand. He took my bags from me and threw them on the couch. "I'm gettin' used to you being around here," he said. "I kinda missed you."

"Nice of you to say so. Maybe I should spend the rest of my life on your couch, keep things simple."

"Hah! You think so? Honey, complications have a way of sneaking up behind you—well, behind anyone really, but especially you. Anyway, you're far too curious to veg out for long." I shrugged, not certain I agreed with him. "C'mon, let's get some coffee poured down you." He put an arm around my shoulder and walked me into the kitchen.

After we'd eaten, we sipped coffee while I told him the latest. Then we called Serge, who promised to zip right over on his bike. Sure enough, ten minutes later, a cheery voice called from the hallway. "Ray-mond? Lil? *C'est moi.* I'm coming in."

Serge was wearing tight black Lycra bicycle shorts and a tank shirt that showed his nicely muscled body. "Ooh-wee, baby," Raymond said, smiling. "They let you out on the streets like this?"

"The construction workers, they *all* stop working to look at me dis morning. I don't know why."

"Well, I do," I said. "Let's see what other excitement you can stir up today." With Raymond quietly listening, Serge told me what he'd found out from the boys. I sat back and thought about it for a few minutes, then made a decision. "Can I talk with these boys myself? Could we meet them somewhere?"

"Sure, why not? Let me call them up—probably they're still asleep."

In less than an hour, I was sitting on a bench in Parc Lafontaine, surrounded by half-naked sun worshipers, neighborhood kids visiting the petting zoo, and old people taking their morning walks. The boys, Gérard and Daniel, arrived after a few minutes on their bikes, greeting Serge like the friend of the family he was. Sleep was still in their eyes, but I could also see they were excited about something. "You're a private detective?" Gérard asked in almost accentless English. "I've always wanted to meet one."

I smiled at him. "You'll probably find me a little bit dull after all those TV detectives." Gérard was cute, tall and reed-thin, with hooded blue eyes. Daniel had blond hair that stuck straight up, with shaved sides, city-sophisticated, but he was soft-spoken and polite. "Let's go sit near the fountain," I said, "away from the crowds."

When we'd settled, I asked them to repeat what they'd told Serge the day before. "Okay. You were working on St-Denis, late Saturday, sweeping up the mess from the festival. Now, what happened?"

Gérard looked at Daniel. "You start," Daniel said. "I'll interrupt if you forget anything."

"Okay." Gérard picked up a little handful of gravel and sifted it from hand to hand while he talked. "We were working like always, cleaning up after the concerts. Mayor Doré doesn't want the city to look messy, and I guess it's cheaper to hire us. Well, Saturday night it was worse than usual and it was getting late, so we were rushing a little. I didn't notice this guy at first, but Daniel did."

Daniel nodded. "He was hanging around, acting a little weird, like he was looking for something."

"Like what?" I asked.

Daniel flashed Gérard a look. "Like drugs, maybe. He seemed nervous."

"Okay," I said. "Then what?"

Gérard picked up the story. "Finally, he walked over to us and asked us how we'd like to make some money. We didn't say anything at first—you know how weirdos come on to you. I figured he'd go away if we ignored him, but then Daniel decided to play along."

I looked at Daniel, raising my eyebrows. He shrugged. "I was curious, I guess."

"So what'd he say?"

"He was looking for some LSD. I didn't have any, and if I had, I wouldn't have sold it to him."

"Why not?"

Gérard blushed a little. "I don't sell drugs, although I have tripped a couple of times. But this guy was *old*. He didn't look like he'd even know what to do with anything if he got it. He had a bad toupee on and everything."

I looked at Serge. Toupee?

"Then what happened?" I asked.

"We told him to try somewhere else, and he walked down toward Berri, near the Métro stop. A couple of minutes later, there he was again, talking to one of those dope dealers who hang around the doorways. He put something in his pocket and then left for good."

I nodded. "Sounds like a dope deal to me. Then what?"

Daniel spoke. "Sunday night, we decided to go with a couple of our chums to get something to drink before work started. One of our friends works as a busboy in the Hôtel Bienvenue—at one of the restaurant/bars upstairs—and he told us he could get us seats by the pool. So we were sitting there having a couple of Cokes when we noticed that same guy sitting at a table, having a drink. He wasn't at the same bar as us; it was the next one down—but still outside, by the pool."

"What'd you do," I asked, "anything?"

Gérard laughed. "We started watching him to see if he looked like he was tripping on anything. We figured it would be fun to see it, as weird and as old as he was. But he just sat there with a drink in front of him. Then, after a while, we noticed that while we were watching him, he seemed to be watching someone else, at the *next* bar down."

"Who?" I asked.

"This couple. The man was real quiet at first and the woman was doing all the talking. Then the man started looking a little wound up or something."

"The second man? The one with the woman?"

He nodded. "Yeah. Then one time, the woman looked over at the guy who'd bought the stuff, and he sort of nodded his head at her, so they must have known each other. The other guy had turned his chair toward the pool meanwhile and had stopped talking again. It seemed weird."

"Then what?"

Daniel gave me an embarrassed look. "It was time to get to work, so we paid up and left. We were laughing, though, trying to imagine the guy tripping his ass off, listening to Ann Murray records or something. He was so uncool."

"And after that?"

"Well," Daniel said, "that musician was killed and it wasn't in the papers on Monday, but it was on the news Monday night." Gérard broke in. "When they showed his picture, I couldn't believe it. I called Daniel and told him to turn on the local news. It was the guy we had seen, all right."

I took a quick breath, then let it out.

"You're sure? Absolutely certain?" I asked.

The teenagers exchanged a brief look, then nodded solemnly. "The second guy was André Ledoux," Gérard said. "He was sitting with the woman, kind of staring at the pool, when we left."

"And the first man?" I asked quietly. "What was he doing, the last time you looked?"

The boys didn't have to think long. "He was watching André Ledoux and the woman, and she was watching him back, it looked like."

Serge cleared his throat. "Dey didn't know if it was somet'ing dey needed to tell somebody about, because not'ing happened in reality, but when I called Gérard's mother . . . well, it gave a good result. Do you agree?"

Not quite, I thought. André was dead.

I got a description of the first man and his toupee and a less-complete description of the woman, whose chair, unfortunately, had been a bit in the shadows. I thanked the boys for the information and advised them to tell the police what they knew, although I had an idea they wouldn't.

We watched them ride away. Serge lit a cigarette, offered me his pack, and we sat there quietly for a few minutes, smoking and thinking.

"Jesus Christ," I finally said. "Those boys were probably the last people to see André alive."

Serge nodded, frowning. "It make you t'ink," he agreed. "No doubt about it, it make you t'ink."

---

"So," I said. "There was a woman with André. There was a man involved, and he had already bought LSD the day before, it looks like. André was full of the stuff when he died. And don't forget, he was choked to death. That takes strength, and although a strong woman could have done it, I'd put my money on the guy with the toupee. Her job was probably to set André up for the kill."

"What about this Tante Eulalie?" Serge asked.

I thought about that until my headache returned. "Well," I said, finally, "let's just skip that part for now. When we figure out what happened to André, his aunt's murder might just fall into place."

Serge nodded. "So who is dis woman?"

I'd been thinking about that, as well. "I suppose she could've been a hooker. Here's the deal: André finally gets a taste of the big time and he decides to do a little celebrating on his own. He's a shy fellow, pretty unsure of himself, so he goes to a hooker, takes her to the kind of fancy joint he's never been able to afford, buys her a drink. Then he intends to pay for some hot sex and make it back to his party at Raymond's restaurant. Only something went wrong. How's that sound to you?" Even as I said the words aloud, I knew they were way off the mark.

Serge and I had been sitting at a sidewalk café on St-Denis for the last hour or so, drinking Perrier with lime, tossing various scenarios around. "It sounds okay, but . . . why would this woman want to kill him? And the LSD had been bought the day before."

"Oh yeah. Right." I thought for another couple of minutes. "What if they didn't have a particular victim in mind? What if they're psychos, or what if they just intended to rob some high roller from out of town? Some scam? What better time than during the Jazz Festival? People here from all over the world and all that."

179

Serge shrugged slightly, then nodded his head. *"C'est possible."* He didn't sound convinced, though, and I couldn't blame him much. Too much coincidence. But there was something else. "We need to find this dope dealer, you know. He could maybe tell us something more about Toupee Head. After all, it wasn't the first time he'd been slipped LSD."

"Aha! It's easy as cake to find a dope dealer, because he wants to be found."

"Pie," I said, "but I got your meaning. Dope dealers have routines, too. Guy stands in a doorway on St-Denis, selling hash and who knows what. Well, he probably does it pretty routinely in that spot so his customers can find him."

Serge nodded. "You let me find him? I know many peoples, and some of them even take LSD still, the younger ones. I myself stopped long time ago."

"Me, too," I said. "I sometimes think my psyche would still enjoy it once a year or so, but then I remember how hard it was on my twenty-five-year-old body. These old bones need all the help they can get."

"Hah! Dese bones look pretty hot to me. And de women check you out when dey pass by."

I stared at him. "They do? How come you notice and I don't?"

He smiled. "Because I notice everyt'ing dat happen, just like animal."

If most people said that to me, I would probably have laughed, but with this man, I didn't even crack a smile. It was true that he seemed to possess a highly developed sense of awareness, almost catlike in its intensity. Yet his presence was light and easy to be around. Raymond had known what he was doing in pairing us up.

"Okay," I said. "You work on the dope-dealer angle and I'll follow up on another possibility I've been considering." I told him what that was. He nodded his head, then smiled.

"*Très intéressant,*" he said almost to himself. "Okey-doke. I meet you later? At Raymond's?"

"Yeah. Raymond's answering machine for getting in touch if you can't make it by suppertime or so—okay?"

"It will not take me long, I t'ink."

I watched him push his bike slowly up the street toward Sherbrooke, thinking that he looked a little like a dope dealer himself. I didn't think he'd have too much trouble. I took a bus up St-Laurent, then walked the rest of the way to Raymond's, where I picked up the keys to his Pontiac. The old gas guzzler's powerful motor started right up and I took pleasure in the smooth ride it gave me all the way over to Waverly. If Lorraine was still there, maybe she had the answers I needed.

---

She came to the door right away, wiping her hands on a dish towel. She was thinner than I'd remembered, although I'd only been gone a couple of days. Her eyes were dry this time, but the circles beneath them told me the young woman had not been having an easy time sleeping since the death of her father.

"Lil! You're back already?"

I looked down and gave my arm a little pinch. "I think it's me," I said. "It looks like me, more or less." I smiled at her. "Got a couple of minutes, we can talk?"

"Oh, sorry. Sure, c'mon in. I was just cleaning up the kitchen. I'm messy and Rubin's neat, so I try to clean up before he gets back from classes."

I walked back with her to the kitchen and perched on a high stool near the butcher-block counter. "Want some coffee?" she asked. "I could make us a cappuccino."

"I never turn down cappuccino," I said. "Sure, if it's not too much trouble."

I waited until she had ground the coffee beans. "Lor-

181

raine, did Ernie West mention to you what had happened down in Maine?"

She frowned. "What do you mean? I know you went down to check something out, that's all."

And then I told her about Aunt Eulalie, the great-aunt she would now never meet. The girl's face paled and she plopped down on another stool across from mine. She bit on her bottom lip, trying not to cry, and I sat there quietly while she took in this latest bit of bad news. She had finally found the other half of her family, and now they were dying in droves.

"I'm sorry to have to tell you," I said. "You didn't know your aunt, so maybe you didn't need to hear this, but, on the other hand, I think I should be straight with you."

She nodded. "What's going on? I don't get it. Everything was going so well."

I didn't have an answer to that. I waited until I'd figured out how to phrase my next question, then took a deep breath and plunged in. "Lorraine, have you been in touch with your mother and stepfather since all this happened?"

She looked puzzled. "Sure. I talked with Mum last night. And Rubin made me call her after my father was killed. Why?"

I dodged her question. "How did your stepfather feel about your getting in touch with André? You said before that he'd been jealous when you were younger and that's why you had lost touch with your father in the first place."

Suddenly, she got my drift. She stood up abruptly, knocking her stool over in the process. "You think my mum and my stepfather killed André and my aunt? What kind of people do you think I come from?"

I held up my hand palm out. "Look, Lorraine, I hated to ask you about them, but I can't overlook any possibility, however slim. Face it—your Canadian family moved when you were little, to keep André away from you. Now you find him, and suddenly he turns up dead. Now I find out that a man and a woman may have been the murderers, so I have to look under every rock. I'm not trying to be cruel, but those are just the facts I have to deal with."

After a minute or two, she sighed and picked up the stool and set it upright. Then she turned her back and fiddled with the coffee machine. The sound of the milk steamer drowned out any possible conversation for another couple of minutes. When she set a cup in front of me and finally looked me in the eye, the pain in her face made her suddenly look old and tired. Good going, Ritchie, I thought. Break what's left of her heart.

I took another deep breath. "Lorraine, it's not that I have any evidence your parents did this. It's just that I have to eliminate any possibilities. Think about this; you'll see it makes sense. That's the only way I can work. Help me here."

"Okay," she said, finally. "But they wouldn't hurt anyone." She looked at me defiantly.

"I'm sure you're right, Lorraine. By the way, does your stepfather wear a toupee by any chance?"

She frowned, looking puzzled. "No, he doesn't. He doesn't have much hair left, but he's not vain about it, either."

"Good. You got a picture of them in your wallet?"

She shook her head. "I've got one on my dresser at home, but . . ."

"That's okay," I said. "What's your stepfather do for a living? And your mom?"

"Dick's a contractor and Mum's a nurse. They work hard."

"I'm sure they do, Lorraine. I'll need their address, just to check things out, but don't worry. I'll be discreet about it."

She gave me their address reluctantly. "They're not there right now, anyway," she said as she handed it over. "They've gone up to the cottage on Georgian Bay, just like every other July. I usually go up for at least a week myself."

I finally convinced her to hand over the phone number and address for their cottage as well and then slunk off, feeling like a coyote caught in the chicken coop. Some days, I swear I'd rather work in a Tastee-Freez.

---

"You think Serge knows anyone at the *Montreal Gazette?*" I asked Raymond in the kitchen of his restaurant. "I need to get hold of a photograph of Lorraine's mother and stepfather."

Raymond was busily removing pecan pies from the oven. He set the last one down to cool and shook his head. "Nah. Serge only reads *La Presse.*" Montreal has three daily newspapers—the *Gazette,* which is the only one written in English, for Anglophones; *La Presse,* the most widely read French paper; and *Le Devoir,* which is French, but with an intellectual bent.

"Why do you need the *Gazette* for that?" Raymond asked.

"Well, if I was to call the paper in Kitchener and ask them to fax me a file photo of Lorraine's parents, I'd need somewhere for them to send it, right?"

"I get it. You're gonna pretend to be a reporter on the *Gazette.* God, you're such a liar, Lil."

I took offense at that. "I'm no such thing! It's just that I need the information quickly, and that's the quickest way."

Raymond smiled sarcastically. "Right. Well, since you didn't ask *me* to help you, then I don't guess you'd be interested in the fact that a good friend of mine is a copy editor at the *Gazette,* would you?"

I looked at him. "You're unbelievable," I said. "You know everybody."

He smiled a genuine smile this time. "I've been here for over twenty years, Lil, don't forget.

"Old boyfriend?" I asked. "I mean, *another* old boyfriend?"

"Could be," he said coyly. "I was quite the heartbreaker in my prime. Anyway, you want me to call him for you? It sounds like a simple thing."

"Would you? That'd be great. I figure the stepfather's a contractor, longtime resident of Kitchener, the mother's a nurse, and at one time or another their picture's probably been in the paper."

"If they're community-minded," Raymond said.

"That's just what I was thinking."

"It's gonna cost you. I just happen to need four cups of finely chopped scallions for garnish. You could be doing that while I talk to Stephen."

I grabbed an apron. "Don't tell him what it's for," I said.

In less than an hour, I had a picture of Dick and Elaine Owens in my hot little hands. In the 1989 staff photo, they smiled brightly from a hot-dog booth they were operating at a citywide fund-raiser to benefit the public library. They were a handsome couple and hardly looked like killers, but then, neither did most convicted murderers. Dick Owens was tall and well built, with thinning dark hair and a waxed salt-and-pepper mustache. His wife was a little plump, with light-colored hair worn short and permed and an open smile. Okay, I thought, squinting at the photo, let's just add four years of hair loss and a toupee to the description the boys gave us.

I couldn't be sure. I called Serge's apartment but only reached his answering machine. Next, I tried Gérard's number and did better—the boy was at home, helping his mother reseed the back lawn. "Want me to meet you somewhere?" he asked a little too hopefully. "I'd be glad to."

"And miss helping your mother? I couldn't do that to you, Gérard. Could I just stop by for a minute to show you a photograph?"

"Sure," he said. "It was worth a try."

I took down the address—a row house on St-Hubert—and realized it wasn't all that far from the restaurant; I could walk it. Too little sleep and too much sitting had stiffened me up, and in lieu of a nice long swim, a stroll would do me good.

"If Serge calls before I get back to the apartment, don't let him get away," I said to Raymond. "I need him for a couple things."

The walk was pleasant, compared with most things I'd been doing for the last few days. The people I met on the street moved quickly and with purpose, even those who, I suspected, were only going as far as their local tavern for a Molson's or two. It would take the heat of Louisiana to slow the French down, I thought.

I checked the address I'd written down and stopped in front of a handsome granite row house in the middle of a long block. Huge old elms shaded most of the buildings on the street and hanging plants and window boxes were everywhere. I climbed to the porch and stooped down to admire a piece of garden statuary that looked vaguely South American in style.

The door opened and a slender, fine-boned, lovely woman stood before me. "Oh," she said, "I didn't hear you knock. I was just checking my mailbox." Her accent and her halting speech told me she didn't normally speak a lot of English.

I smiled at her. "Actually, I hadn't gotten around to knocking quite yet. I was admiring this piece here." I pointed to the statuary. "It's wonderful."

Delight spread across her face and into her dark eyes. "I'm so glad you like it," she said. "It's my work. I'm a *sculpteur*—in English, sculp-tor? Is it right, how I say this?" She hesitated.

"Perfect," I said. "Serge should have told me more about you. This is beautiful work." I held out my hand and introduced myself. "Oh yes." She smiled. "That Serge, he's something. He is my friend since twenty-five years. And he's been like an uncle to my boy Gérard."

"I'd gotten that impression," I said. I told her what I wanted and she took me out to the backyard, where Gérard

186

stood, miserably leaning on a rake, staring down at the ground. His hair was sticking to his forehead, his shirt sweat-drenched.

"That's okay, Gérard." His mother laughed. "Sit down in the shade and I'll get us something to drink."

The woman disappeared, and I squelched an impulse to watch her go. Gérard sat down. I took the chair next to him, pulling the copy of the photograph out of my pocket. "Ever seen these people before?" I asked.

The boy held it in his hands for a couple of minutes, frowning in concentration. Then he handed it back. "Nope. At least I don't think so. Should I know them?"

"Imagine this guy with a bad toupee. Think about the woman you saw by the pool. Take your time."

He looked at the photo again, then handed it back. "No way," he said. "The other guy was all different, older and uglier. The woman was taller and not as nice-looking."

I sat there and thought for a minute or two. Then Gérard's mother, whose name was Jocelyne, came back carrying iced mineral water in tall glasses with sprigs of fresh mint, and for a few minutes I indulged myself in idle, pleasant conversation.

On the way back to Raymond's apartment, my mind wandered this way and that. I wondered why I was always drawn to settled-down women whose lives were seemingly already full. I thought about the couple in Kitchener, Ontario, whose lives had just been altered by the brief reemergence and death of an ex-husband and father. I thought about a daughter who had come so very close to what she needed, only to have it ripped away like an unopened present.

I'd finally satisfied myself that the Owenses had nothing to do with the killings of André and Eulalie. But if they hadn't done it, then who had?

I climbed the stairs to Raymond's place, moving more slowly than I had all day.

# CHAPTER EIGHTEEN

S e r g e
showed up before I'd even taken my shoes off. I told him what
I'd learned from Gérard and he listened closely, tapping his
fingers excitedly on the arm of his chair. "How about you?"
I asked. "Find our dealer?"

He nodded, smiling from ear to ear. "I find 'im with no
trouble. De second dealer I talk to."

"Great," I said. "What's his story?" I leaned back on the
sofa, wriggling my toes.

"Well, to begin, he doesn't like to say, but then I convince him I'm not police. Hah! Me police?" He looked at me,
offended. "I don't even like police, I tell him. Except Sting."

Raymond guffawed from the next room. Ignoring him,
I said, "So what happened?"

"De dealer—'is name is Paul—'e told me what de man
look like. Six foot two and with small, small eyes. 'E's maybe
fifty. And when he talk—big American accent." Serge paused,
watching my reaction. " 'e has also, how you say . . . *postiche?*"

"A toupee?"

"Yes, he is wearing a *toupet*, dark brown. Oh yes. He is
very, very, eh, *nerveux.*"

"An American," I said. "Interesting. What did he buy?
How did he ask for it?"

" 'E buy t'ree 'it of LSD. 'E say 'e want to give a little
surpreeze to a friend."

188

I snorted. "Some surprise. The first of several, I'd say."

He nodded. " 'E say de man 'ave weird vibe, not like cop, but weird. Didn't want to pay what Paul ask. Try to get for less. Finally, 'e pay and den go off, like dat."

I thought for a few minutes. "What kind of weird vibes? He was nervous—that makes sense. Anything else?"

"Paul t'ink he very mean guy. At same time, de guy act like 'e t'ink 'imself better dan Paul, or somet'ing like dat."

"Interesting. Anything else?"

Serge shook his head. "I pay de dealer twenty bucks and I go."

"I'll give that back to you in a minute," I said. "That was great work, Serge. Thanks. I'm not sure what it means yet, but at least it lets Lorraine's mother and stepfather off the hook for good. And Ernie West and Al Sandberg."

He frowned. "You t'ink his friends could do a t'ing like dat?"

"Nah, not really," I said. "But you have to consider everyone who knew the victim. And like the man said, Toupee Head was an American."

"With a bald head."

"Yeah." I nodded. "Or he wanted his own hair hidden."

"Whew. I did not t'ink about dat."

I looked at my watch. "I've gotta make a couple of calls before I do anything else. You busy tonight?"

"I'll be at my place, watching video. You need me, you call."

I said I would and gave him a twenty-dollar bill. I spent the next hour writing down what I'd uncovered so far, not wanting to forget any details, no matter how small. Then I helped Raymond polish off some restaurant leftovers for dinner and called Ernie West, who would be driving back to Lewiston with Al in the morning. Next, I phoned Lorraine to let her know her mother and stepfather were in the clear. The young woman was relieved, I could tell, and I apologized for

189

causing her needless worry. She, too, would be leaving Montreal in the next day or so.

It took me three hours and six unanswered phone calls to reach Molly. "Lil!" she said breathlessly. "I'm just coming in the door. I was going to call you."

"You got something for me?" I asked.

"Yeah, though I'm not sure what it means. Bart checked out that phone number for you, and you'll never guess what it was."

I held my breath. "What was it?"

"The Church of Redemption," she said. "The headquarters number . . . in Waterville."

"Huh?" I frowned into the phone. "You sure?" This didn't make any sense at all.

"Yep. Checked and rechecked."

What did this mean? The Church of Redemption was a huge right-wing religious organization, headed by a preacher named Curtis Haskell. He was famous throughout Maine for his bigoted and organized antigay rhetoric, as well as his vehement opposition to abortion, even in the case of rape. But who would be calling his headquarters from Montreal? And why? And how could the matchbook have ended up in Eulalie's house?

"Thanks, Molly," I said. "I've got to think about this a little. If I need to call you back, how late will you be up?"

"Just call if you need, Lil. I don't have anything in the morning tomorrow, so I'll probably stay up, see who's on 'Letterman.' "

I hung up and added this new bit of information to my report. In the morning, I'd call the headquarters myself and see what I could find out. Meanwhile, my tiredness was catching up with me, so I hung around the apartment, watching TV with Raymond—a charming little National Film Board movie set in Nova Scotia, followed by the local news. Then he flipped around the dial until he settled in on his favorite late-night entertainment.

I sat up abruptly. "That's the guy!" I said. "That's Curtis Haskell, that bigot preacher from Maine!"

"Really?" Raymond stretched out on the floor. "Don't you just love him? I used to watch old 'Rockford' reruns until I discovered this guy. He's great, although I can't believe he takes himself this seriously."

I looked at him. "Where you been, anyway? This guy is dead serious. He's caused a lot of harm to both women and gays with his big mouth."

"Aw, shucks," Raymond said. "Just when I was getting into this stuff."

We watched it for a while, anyway. I'd known he was on late-night TV, but I didn't have cable, so this was the first time I'd actually seen his full performance. I'd seen glimpses of him on the news, but this was different. The camera panned the audience frequently, and I was amazed at the obvious sincerity on the faces of his followers, who ranged from teenagers to the elderly. An 800 number flashed on the screen intermittently, inviting home viewers to send in money orders or checks to help with the expenses of the ministry.

"How much d'you suppose a guy like this makes a year?" Raymond asked. "This audience looks poor enough."

"Huh. I wonder how much money they had before this jackass got his mitts into them."

We watched to the end as Haskell worked his audience like a yo-yo. He ranted and raved from the pulpit, reminding the old people that they were unworthy of heaven and the young that they had no right to a better life. They were sinners and would suffer accordingly. Then, lest he lose his audience, he called out his Redemption Singers, a seven-member choir whose music softened the harsh message somewhat. Then the

800 number flashed on again, followed by an offer for miracle healings.

"This isn't religion," I told Raymond. "This is a scam."

"I'm shocked," Raymond said. "Tell me it's not true."

I threw a pillow at him. "Look, we both come from Bible-banger country, but there's a big difference between somebody like Billy Graham and this sucker here."

"Yeah, but there're so many televangelists like this guy Haskell, they kind of overshadow the real thing."

"But they're so phony!" I wailed.

"To you, my dear," Raymond said, "to you."

Raymond finally turned in for the night. I lay on my sofa in the dark, watching the headlights reflect on the ceiling as an occasional car passed by. I drifted off to sleep. But suddenly, I bolted up as if from a nightmare, my heart pounding.

What was it that Aunt Eulalie had said to me on her deathbed? I replayed as much of our conversation as I could. *"Y'ont tué mon beau gars."* "They killed my beautiful boy."

Then I'd asked her who had assaulted her and she'd replied, *"Y'est à la TV."* "He's on TV."

Who? I'd asked, and she'd answered, *"C't un démon!"* "He's a demon!"

She'd seen him on TV. If these hadn't been the ravings of a dying woman, then Eulalie had tried to tell me her killer's name.

Was it Haskell? I got up and paced the floor as quietly as I could in my bare feet, sweat pouring from my body. Then I called the loft, in case Ernie West hadn't yet left for home. It took him a while to pick up, and at least another half minute to mumble a sleep-laden hello.

"Get up," I said. "Put on a pot of coffee, because I'm coming over. We've gotta talk about something."

I heard his sigh of exhaustion, but I didn't care. "Just do it," I said. "You can catch up later." Then I hung up.

Next I called Dorval Airport and booked the first available seat on the morning flight to Boston, which would connect up with a commuter shuttle to Portland. From there, I would rent a car. Someone had gotten away with two murders so far, but if I had my way about it, their murdering days were over.

---

I walked into the Parker-Noyes Funeral Home at a little past four o'clock. A quick call to Father Jean-Pierre had told me the time and place of André's wake and Eulalie's, as well. The old woman's body was in the Lewiston funeral home, one room away from her favorite nephew's. The irony of this setup was almost more than I could take—the two relatives whose closeness in life led to their closeness in death—but then, I hadn't been the one doing the planning.

The priest was just inside the front door, speaking with someone I took to be the director. "Miss Ritchie!" he said, smiling. "I'm glad you could make it. I'm sure both André and poor Eulalie would've wanted you here."

"How can I not be here?" I said, looking around me. "Who else is here?"

The priest lowered his voice. "Just Lucie and her husband and a few relatives from up in the County. And Mrs. Ledoux."

I nodded. "You work out that little problem with Irene about where the funeral's being held?"

"Oh, goodness yes. She just didn't realize we Catholics would be so upset, especially since her husband wasn't much of a churchgoing man." He rubbed his hands rapidly together and smiled. "You know—once a Catholic."

"That's what I've always heard," I said. "Of course, I know some ex-Catholics who are Buddhists, and even a couple who are Jehovah's Witnesses, plus a few who say they're recovering."

193

The priest frowned, raising his eyebrows in irritation. "Really? Well, of course nothing's a hundred percent nowadays, is it? People are easily confused."

More people had been filing in as we talked and I couldn't help noticing that almost every mourner signed both books. I walked into Eulalie's viewing room, where people stood around in groups of two or three, speaking in the hushed tones reserved for such venues. I was greeted politely by several, who identified themselves as relatives or neighbors of the old woman. Finally, I had a moment to myself and I walked up to the casket and cautiously looked in.

Eulalie would've hated her makeup job and her hairdo, as well, I thought. The old woman's practical bun had been turned into a swirl of blue-tinted and teased hair and the bright rouge and even brighter lips belonged to someone maybe, but not to the Eulalie I had briefly known. "Sorry about this," I whispered. "I'd 've run a comb through your hair and left it at that."

Then I walked next door to face what was left of André. Lucie stood in a small receiving line in the farthest corner of the room, along with Irene and some other relatives I didn't recognize. People were pouring in now, pumping hands like politicians just before election day. Ernie had finally arrived, wearing a black suit that looked brand-new. Al, he whispered, would be along as soon as he could get it together. The drummer had attended almost no funerals in his life and was reluctant to start now with that of a friend and close colleague.

I made my way over to Lucie and offered my condolences. The young woman's face was changed by grief. I hoped the sadness in her eyes would go away in time. She squeezed my hand hard. "I never knew anything could hurt like this," she said quietly. "But I guess the thing to do is to honor my brother's life by living well myself. That's what Father says, anyway. Not that it's going to be easy."

194

"You'll do fine, Lucie. At least you know your brother loved you."

She nodded, suddenly overcome. When another mourner stepped up, I patted her shoulder and moved on.

Next, I spoke briefly to Irene. André's wife looked tired and worn, with dark circles under her eyes, her face haggard from lack of sleep. She'd been crying and her makeup was slightly tear-smeared. "Thanks so much for coming," she said. "This is a hard day for us all, but it helps to know that people cared so much for André."

"He was a sweet person." I still felt uncomfortable speaking of André in the past tense, but I knew I'd have to start sometime. "I understand there's to be a double funeral Mass tomorrow at the cathedral."

She nodded. "Father Jean-Pierre convinced me it's the right thing to do, with his Catholic upbringing and all."

Just then, a heavily perfumed woman lunged at Irene, engulfing her in a bosom-rich hug, and I stepped aside. I stood around for a while, then said my good-byes to the family and to the priest. I saved Ernie for last. Al still hadn't shown up, and now I wondered whether he would.

"Don't you breathe a word," I said to him now. "I'm handling this." He nodded, although he looked more than a little doubtful.

I spent the next two hours sitting outside in my rental car, watching people come and go. The Honda was fairly comfortable at first, but soon I began thinking of it as my prison cell. I knew what I had to do and I was tired of waiting.

At half past eight or so, the last mourners trailed out of the funeral home and I ducked down in my seat just in case. When the car I was waiting for pulled out, I counted to ten and eased in behind it, careful to leave plenty of distance between us. The driver made one stop—at a phone booth outside a convenience store. Luckily, there was room in front of a fire hydrant and I ducked in, sweat pouring into my eyes.

I sat there, breathing deeply, until the car started up again, then took up where we'd left off, part cat, part mouse. There wasn't much traffic, so I hung back a little more than I normally would have, playing it safe.

Finally, we'd reached our destination and the driver pulled into a parking space along the edge of a yard. When the lights came on inside the house, I waited again, and a second car arrived. As soon as its driver had entered the house, I said my prayers and checked my small voice-activated tape recorder for the umpteenth time, finally sticking it into my shirt pocket. Taking another couple of deep, calming breaths and feeling no better for it at all, I forced myself to get out of the car.

I could see moving shadows through the curtains. I tried to peek into a living room window, but it was a little too high, so I continued to the back of the house, where the shrubbery would give me at least some cover. I stood near the back steps for a full ten minutes, listening, before I finally tiptoed onto the porch. No time like the present, I thought.

I put my ear to the back door and heard murmurs almost completely out of hearing range coming from the front of the house. Holding my breath, I turned the knob once, carefully. The door was unlocked. I waited another minute or two, allowing my breathing to slow down, then I pushed the door open an inch or two at a time until I had no choice but to enter the house. I closed the door behind me as quietly as I could.

Urgently checking my surroundings, I found myself standing in a long hallway, near a utility room and half bath. Step by step, I inched along, past what looked to be a sewing room and then a spare bedroom. The voices were louder now. They came from what I thought was the kitchen. I heard what sounded like a whiskey bottle being uncapped and I reached again into my front pocket to check my recorder. It was on.

Then abruptly, footsteps started coming my way. I ducked into the room to my left, the master bedroom, by the looks of it. There was a silly pink satin spread on the double bed. Someone had moved across the hall to the living room. In a matter of seconds, a second person followed.

I took off my sneakers and socks, then peered out into the hall. It was clear. Slowly and stealthily, I crept toward the voices until they were as clear as they were going to get. Then, closing my eyes to fight down panic and the fear of being discovered, I listened.

"I told you we didn't have to kill him. That's why I slipped him the drugs. It worked once, it would work again."

I heard the sound of ice cubes being swished around in a glass, then a heavy sigh. "Honey, I explained it and I explained it. After all, he knew about the first time, and he'd told that aunt of his. It's not our fault. It's like he made us do it."

So André had killed himself? I suppressed a snort of contempt.

"But . . ." I heard a sniffle. "Well, I guess you're right. I had no idea his daughter would show up out of nowhere and that that would make him want to keep the family together. I never thought of that."

"There, there," he soothed. "It's all over now. He'll be buried and gone, and so will the old gal; then we can be the next Jim and Tammy Faye, doing God's work just the way we planned it all along. But we're gonna be a whole lot smarter than they were. It's like I said, it's for the greater good. Think of it this way—maybe we just fought the devil and won."

"Not yet, you haven't," I said, walking silently into the room. "Could be, you just yanked on the wrong tail."

They looked at me stupidly, in disbelief.

"Hi, Irene," I said. "Why don't you introduce me to your boyfriend."

They looked at each other and then back at me. "Your wig looks like shit," I said to the preacher evenly, smiling a bit. "You really should do something about that rug."

The old rage had returned and I suddenly noticed I'd stopped feeling nervous. We were still playing cat and mouse, but this time things had changed: I was the cat.

# CHAPTER NINETEEN

■ ■ ■ ■ ■ ■ ■ ■ ■ ■ ■ ■ ■ ■ ■ ■

I r e n e
slumped down on the sofa, all the blood suddenly draining
from her face, leaving it almost as waxy pale as the people
she'd helped put in the funeral home. "It's not what you
think," she said.

"Oh, I wouldn't bet on that, Irene. At the moment, I'm
thinking some pretty dark thoughts, and I've got good information, too."

The preacher broke in. "Who the hell is this woman?" he
shouted, incredulous. "What's she doing here?" He looked
from Irene to me, then back to Irene.

"I'm the woman who figured out your little game," I
said. "And I know who you are, Reverend Haskell. I've been
itching to meet you for quite a while. I just didn't think it
would happen in the house of the man you killed."

Irene sat up a bit. "This is that detective I told you
about," she said to Haskell.

The preacher took in the information, then shifted his
weight slightly on the plastic-covered sofa. "I don't have to sit
here and take this," he said belligerently.

"Yes, you do." I kept my eyes on him.

"I want to call my lawyer, then. At least you have to read
me my rights or something."

"Like hell I do," I said. "I'm a private eye, and I don't
have to do a damned thing I don't want to do. This is per-

sonal—no phone calls, no lawyers. It's just between you and me, and if I were you, I'd be plenty worried." He started to get up, then changed his mind.

"Don't make me shoot you," I said, " 'cause I'm not sure that I'd mind doing it all that much." I pulled out the new handgun I'd purchased in a Portland gun shop earlier in the day for just a little over two hundred dollars. It was a nice little Smith & Wesson copy—A J-Frame Taurus Model 85 with a two-inch barrel. It had fit snugly into the waistband of my jeans.

Irene's eyes widened with fear, but the preacher tried a new tack. "Look, I'm sure we've only misunderstood each other. Let's not jump to conclusions." He tried for a smile and missed.

"Sure," I said, "I can be reasonable. But suppose you tell me what really happened."

He moved again and I clicked off the safety, aiming the gun right at his chest. He looked at me sharply, then shifted his legs. "Can't I just stand up or something?" he whined. "I can't think sitting down. Honest to God, that's true. My legs are too long."

"We could try having you lie facedown. Would that be better?" I heard the sound of my own voice, and there was something in it I didn't entirely recognize. Irene heard it, too, because she poked the preacher with an elbow. "She's the one with the gun, Curtis, and I think she'd like to use it. Just do what she says."

I leaned back against the doorjamb, wanting to keep some distance between them, particularly the preacher and me. I lowered my right hand, the one with the gun, leaving the safety off. The Taurus would get heavy quickly and it would take me only a split second to raise it and shoot if the need arose.

"So tell me how this happened," I said. "The whole story."

200

Irene looked at Haskell, who never took his small eyes off me. Serge's dope dealer had been right—he did have small eyes, and he was mean. I raised the gun again, pointing it directly at him. "I can use this if you'd rather, but what I'd prefer is to hear the truth."

He gave me a long, calculating look, then turned toward Irene. "You start," he said. "This damned woman's crazy as a loon."

Irene sat there for half a minute, then sighed. "How'd you figure out it was us?" she asked.

"I found the matchbook from the Montreal hotel at Eulalie Tremblay's house—the one with that phone number written inside it. When I had the number checked out and found it belonged to Haskell's right-hand man, I had a pretty good idea." I looked at Haskell now. "You'd missed an appointment and you had to call him to smooth things over. I had that checked out. But you dropped that little piece of evidence in Eulalie's house. How's that?"

Nobody was answering. "Then, I made Ernie West tell me all about you, Irene. He'd been protecting André, in his way, by not spilling the beans about your relationship. You were just plain mean to that man, hiding his instruments, harassing him before performances. Ernie said he and André's other friends kept hoping things would improve. He was just so glad finally to see André with someone, *anyone*. Then when I asked him on a hunch where you worked, he told me you worked for the Reverend here"—I waved the gun at Haskell—"well, that pretty much did it."

Irene swallowed a few times. "What parts don't you know?" she asked in a small voice.

"Plenty, but let's start with this: How did you slip the acid to André the first time? And why?"

She shrugged. "To keep him in line, more or less. When he was on heroin or whiskey, I didn't have a piece of trouble with him. But right after he went to rehab, he was a handful.

I wanted him to mess up in front of his precious public so I could get a divorce and marry Curtis." She sneaked a look at the preacher, whose eyes were riveted on me.

"Irene, anyone can get a divorce. You didn't need to go that far."

She shook her head. "You don't understand. There were things that would come out, and I couldn't be messed up in any scandal. I could divorce a man who was a druggie, though, and hold my head up high afterward for leaving him."

"What kind of things would've come out?" I asked quietly.

She shrugged. I raised my gun hand again and Haskell elbowed her ribs. "For Christ's sake, you might as well tell her. We got nothing to lose."

She sighed. "A while back, I was arrested a couple of times for prostitution. That was before I found Jesus, but people wouldn't understand that necessarily."

I laughed. "Sister, I'd have hated to see you before you got religion, if this is what you're like with it."

She frowned, tossed her head, and arranged her mouth in a pout. "So who did you get to slip him the LSD the first time?"

"Just a guy I know. Met him at a sex shop."

"Let me guess," I said. "He's an ex-john or something and you paid him with cash."

She nodded, finally getting into the story. "Yeah, but he tried to get some more money out of me afterward and I told him to stuff it. So the creep went to André and told him all about the LSD."

I whistled softly. "So *that's* what scared André into ducking out of town after having stolen his sister's money. His nearest and dearest was out to get him." I thought about it for a few seconds. "Did you know he found out?"

She shook her head. "Not until I talked to him in Montreal." She glanced at the preacher, who ignored her, no doubt having plenty on his mind. "He told me he forgave me for slipping him that dose and for the other things that had happened. Said he knew he hadn't been a good enough husband and he wanted us back together, to try again. Said that since he'd found his daughter again, he finally understood where we'd gone wrong. Said he'd explained it all to his aunt that morning and was disappointed that she'd tried to talk him out of meeting me that night. He was all excited about it. Of course, that was the last thing I needed. And that damned girl showing up out of the blue! It was all bad luck."

"What a piece of work you are," I said. "He was scared of you and you knew it. But he was still ready to come back for more."

She shrugged again, then glanced at the preacher. I was getting irritated. "It's true, we did have some fights in the past, but I was bigger than him." She laughed, a coarse bark. "Didn't I blacken that man's eye a time or two, Curtis?"

I wasn't laughing back, and neither, I noticed, was the preacher. "That's one of the many things that would've spoiled your chances of being the next Tammy Faye Bakker, isn't it?"

"I guess so."

"So since Aunt Eulalie knew about this shit, she would have talked to the police, right? That's why you beat her to death. You had to cut your losses." I looked at Haskell, who was now starting to shift his weight again. He wasn't giving up.

"Look," he said. "I'm sorry about the old gal, but my hands were tied. She was the only one who could connect us to Montreal."

Either the room was getting hotter or my temperature was rising. "Killing André was your idea, I suppose." I glared at Haskell. "Were you the one who choked him, too?"

He smiled for the first time and I caught a glimpse of the

man's real ugliness. "With his own guitar strap," he said. "I think a fan had just given it to him."

I'd had about enough of the two of them. I edged a little farther into the room and approached the end table where the telephone sat. Picking up the receiver, I dialed a number I'd memorized earlier. "I've got their confession," I said. "Come on over, and bring some cuffs." I hung up.

I looked over at Haskell, whose face was suddenly bright red. "You've caused a lot of harm in this part of the world," I said. "Maybe it's time you were on the receiving end to balance things out a little. How's life in Thomaston sound?"

He stared at me, his eyes full of hatred. "What are you, anyway, some kind of pinko dyke?"

I stared right back at him. "As a matter of fact, yeah, I am. And I'm a pretty good citizen, too. I'm bringing you down all the way, mister, and it's gonna be a pleasure."

"I'm not goin' to any state prison," he growled. "I've got plans."

Suddenly, Irene seemed to collapse, slumping down, her head near her knees. "Oh God!" she moaned. "Why did this happen to me? It's all that stupid girl's fault!"

The preacher leaned over as if to comfort her, and I followed his movement with the gun.

He'd decided on a new approach. So fast, I could hardly follow his movements, he pulled out a knife, and now he held it to Irene's throat. "Put the goddamned gun down," he said, "or I'll slit her from ear to ear."

Irene's eyes grew huge, showing her shock and disbelief. She swallowed hard a couple of times and appeared to be trying to speak, but no sounds would come out of her mouth. I decided to bluff it.

"You forget that I'm pretty mad at Irene. Maybe it would be the best thing," I said as evenly as I could.

In one quick movement, the preacher was on his feet, dragging Irene up with him, then shoving her toward me with his considerable adrenalized strength. She slammed full force into my abdomen and chest. I almost blacked out under the impact. Stumbling backward through the doorway, I struggled desperately to regain my balance and shake off her weight, but a spike heel connected with my bare foot, injecting a flow of pain, and I fell, dragging her down with me. I heard the gun go off as it hit the floor.

Now Haskell was barreling toward us, his eyes glazed over, and I realized he was coming for the Taurus, which lay just out of my reach, on the edge of the kitchen floor. I attempted to roll over and reach the gun, but Irene's weight was pinning me down. Frantically kicking out at her with all my strength, I soon heard a groan that told me I'd connected. As she rolled off me, I lifted myself up enough to lunge toward the gun, stretching my fingers all the way out until I touched the cool metal of the barrel. In a flash, I turned it around, cocked the hammer, and prepared to fire.

Just as I started to pull the trigger, I heard a loud pounding noise, followed by the sound of splintering wood. The front door collapsed. A voice shouted, "Freeze!" and heavy boots rushed toward us. I caught a split-second glimpse of Haskell's face that told me he still hadn't given up. He wheeled around, heading for the back door. Then there was a shot, followed by a thud.

It was over. I sat up, pulled myself against the nearest wall, drawing my knees to my chest, and looked up into Bart's smiling face. "Nice going," he said. "We just winged him. Got the tape?"

I shook my head until it rattled. "Took you guys long enough," I finally muttered, reaching in my pocket for the recorder, which, miraculously, was still in one piece, and handing it over.

Irene was being helped to her feet by two big state cops. I looked at Bart. "Buddies of yours?"

He nodded. One of them began to read her her rights

from a little card while the other prepared to put on the cuffs. Standing there, she seemed smaller than she had just a few minutes earlier. For a moment, our eyes locked.

I nudged Bart. "Can I say something to her before they take her out of here?"

He whispered something to the state boys and they nodded and stepped aside, looking back at me with curiosity. I stood up, feeling shakier than I'd expected, and tested myself for injuries. I was okay. Down the hall, cops still swarmed all over Haskell, who was sitting on the floor. At least he wasn't dead, I thought. He'd live to enjoy prison life, after all.

I walked over to Irene and again our eyes met. "I didn't really want him to kill you," I said.

She nodded. "I know it," she said gruffly. "You did what you had to do."

I thought about that for a minute. "Yeah, I guess I did."

Her eyes veered off toward Haskell and then her gaze swept past me, past Bart, past the state cops, and into the remainder of her empty life. She looked down toward her feet, defeated and alone. But I hadn't finished.

"Irene, do you know what you did when you killed André?" I asked softly, standing close to her now. She looked at me blankly, probably still in shock.

"When you killed that beautiful, trusting human being, you killed his God-given gift, too. It died with him, Irene, and now we don't have it anymore, and we sorely need it. You killed pure and sweet music, and no one—*no one*—has that right. I want to make sure you understand that." She stared back at me, and although I could have imagined it, I thought I saw some kind of recognition in her eyes.

I'd finally said what I had to say. It wouldn't bring back André, or Eulalie, or the music, but I had to say it anyway.

I left her standing there, walked out onto the porch, and

sat down heavily on the top step. For a while I stared at nothing, then I looked around, taking in the quiet tree-lined street and, above that, the skyful of stars. I took some deep breaths and let the cool Maine air calm me down.

"So how come you didn't suspect Irene all along?"

Ernie cleared his throat. "That's my fault. If I'd told Lil about the times I'd heard her shriek at him, or even some little things I'd seen, well . . ." He shrugged. "Maybe he'd still be alive." He raised his eyes from the Dos Equis he was holding, and I could see he had a long way yet to go. Grief heals when it heals, I thought, and not a minute before.

It had been over a month since the death of André Ledoux and I'd decided to give myself a little birthday present. I'd called Ernie and asked him to the house for dinner, without mentioning the significance of the date. Then Molly and I had spent all day cooking in my portable genuine Texas oil-drum barbecue pit, smoking the brisket slowly, the way my friend Robert, the Austin Barbecue King, had taught me to do. Molly had brought her famous potato salad and I'd simmered the pinto beans the day before. Now I set out the dish of homemade pickled jalapeños—with basil, oregano, sliced onions, and garlic, the way they are prepared in some parts of Mexico—and let my eyes inspect the table. It looked pretty good to me.

"You guys need anything else? You got beer? More napkins? You're gonna need 'em."

"Just bring the roll of paper towels over," Molly said. "These smells are driving me crazy. It's a good thing I starved myself all day."

I looked at Ernie. "She didn't, really. She's been doing what she calls 'just picking,' which only means that she didn't actually sit down in a chair to eat. Don't let her fool you." I raised my beer. "Here's to good food and good friends, wherever they may be."

We toasted and then dug into the food. It wouldn't put the Salt Lick in Dripping Springs, Texas, out of business, but here in Maine, it was the best we'd be likely to find. The heap of used paper towels was proof of this.

I pushed myself back from the table and Littlefield jumped into my lap, sniffing and licking my fingers so frantically that even Ernie laughed. I sighed. "Might as well just give him some barbecue, if it'll save my skin." I sliced off a little meat for him and set it in his dish on the floor. My guests watched in amazement as he ate. "When's the last time you fed this guy?" Molly asked. "December?"

"Cats lie," I said. "He ate an hour ago, but maybe he was 'just picking,' too."

Ernie had been quiet during dinner. "I was wondering about something. Why didn't you just have it out with Irene at the funeral home? How could you just talk to her like there was nothing else going on? Then later, it was so dangerous, what you did. You could've gotten killed before the cops even got to the house."

I'd been thinking about that a lot. "I didn't have any hard evidence linking Irene and Haskell to the killing, not really. I had to catch them together. But I wanted to speak with her at the funeral home, just to get a sense of where she was coming from. She seemed genuinely upset—she'd been crying and she was shaky—which, to me, meant she'd have to stick close to her boyfriend in order to keep things together. Now I know that she hadn't wanted to kill André—she'd only wanted him to agree to a divorce—but the preacher had pushed her in that direction. He was afraid André would spill the beans."

209

"What about Aunt Eulalie?" Molly asked. "Did Irene take part in that?"

"Who knows," I said. "According to her, she only went with Haskell to show him the house, then waited in the car. That, of course, makes her an accessory."

"At least they're both locked up," Ernie said.

"Yeah, there is that."

But we all knew that it wasn't enough. We sat in silence for a couple of minutes, watching the cat lick his dish, then the floor around it. Now if he'd just do windows, I thought, smiling to myself.

Molly got up and started stacking the dirty dishes in the sink. "You know," I said to Ernie, "I just didn't want André's wake or his funeral to be touched by this nastiness any more than could be helped. I think that's the real reason I dealt with Irene on my own, and the preacher, too. André's life had been so hard and he'd had so little satisfaction. I wanted the people who really loved him to be able to say good-bye in peace, with dignity. He deserved so much more, but that's all I could give him in the end."

Ernie's eyes filled up and I reached across the table to hold his big hand. Molly discreetly left the kitchen, and after a minute or two, I heard her searching through my record albums for something to play. Then Aretha's "Do Right Woman" drifted into the room, and for a couple of minutes I closed my eyes and let the Queen of Soul speak for us all.

"You couldn't save him either, Ernie. You tried by protecting him in all the ways you could think of, but the die had been cast. It was too late. Now you have to pick up your own life, when you can. That's the best way of honoring your friend. This is something I've learned the hard way, believe me, but it's as true as it is painful."

We spent the rest of the evening listening to music and talking. Ernie was a sweet guy and I intended to keep up with him and make sure he was okay. I'd check on him when he

210

returned from his tour with Lee Wilder and his visit with Lorraine. Molly played deejay, moving from Aretha to Otis Redding to Marvin Gaye, dancing by herself from time to time. Now that she was no longer dating the lawyer, she had energy to burn. Before leaving, Ernie had written out a generous check for the work I had done on André's case. I hadn't wanted to take it, but it was the way I made my living, after all, so I'd finally given in.

After we watched Ernie drive away, Molly and I went back to the music, switching styles, finally ending up with Randy Newman's *Good Old Boys,* one of our old favorites. We sang along with "Rednecks" loudly enough for Littlefield to run up to the attic to escape the noise. When we came to the line "We don't know our ass from a hole in the ground," we sang even louder through our laughter, and for just a flash, it was 1974, the music was new, and we were young.

I had just turned forty.

I was lucky. There would be new songs.